THE QUICKIE

JAMES PATTERSON
&
MICHAEL LEDWIDGE

THE QUICKIE

headline

First published in Great Britain in 2007
by HEADLINE PUBLISHING GROUP

1

Cataloguing in Publication Data is available from the British Library

ISBN 978 0 7553 3570 1 (Hardback)
ISBN 978 0 7553 3571 8 (Trade paperback)

Typeset in Palatino Light by Palimpsest Book Production Ltd,
Grangemouth, Stirlingshire

Printed and bound in Australia by Griffin Press

Headline's policy is to use papers that are natural, renewable
and recyclable products and made from wood grown in sustainable forests.
The logging and manufacturing processes are expected to conform
to the environmental regulations of the country of origin.

HEADLINE PUBLISHING GROUP
A division of Hachette Livre UK Ltd
338 Euston Road
London NW1 3BH

www.headline.co.uk
www.hodderheadline.com

To John and Joan Downey – thanks for everything

PROLOGUE

NOBODY REALLY LIKES SURPRISES

One

I knew this was a really terrific idea, if I didn't say so myself, surprising Paul for lunch at his office down on Pearl Street.

I'd made a special trip into Manhattan and had put on my favorite 'little black dress.' I looked moderately ravishing. Nothing that would be out of place at the Mark Joseph Steakhouse, and one of Paul's favorite outfits, too, the one he usually chose if I asked him, 'What should I wear to this thing, Paul?'

Anyway, I was excited, and I'd already spoken to his assistant, Jean, to make sure that he was there – though I hadn't alerted her about the surprise. Jean was Paul's assistant after all, not mine.

And then, there was Paul.

As I rounded the corner in my Mini Cooper, I saw him leaving his office building, walking with a twenty-something blonde woman.

Paul was leaning in very close to her, chatting, laughing in a way that instantly made me feel very ill.

She was one of those bright, shiny beauties you're more likely to see in Chicago or Iowa City. Tall, hair like platinum silk. Cream-colored skin that looked just about perfect from this distance. Not a wrinkle or blemish.

She wasn't completely perfect, though. She tripped a Manolo

on a street plate as she and Paul were getting into a taxi, and as I watched Paul gallantly catch hold of the pink cashmere on her anorexic elbow, I felt like someone had hammered a cold chisel right into the center of my chest.

I followed them. Well, I guess *followed* is too polite. I stalked them.

All the way up to Midtown, I stayed on that taxi's bumper like we were connected by a tow hook. When the cab suddenly pulled up in front of the entrance to the St Regis Hotel, on East 55th Street, and Paul and the woman stepped out smiling, I felt an impulse rush from the lizard part of my brain to my right foot, which was hovering over the accelerator. Then Paul took her arm. A picture of both of them sandwiched between the storied hotel's front steps and the hood of my baby-blue Mini flashed through my mind.

Then it was gone, and so were they, and I was left sitting there crying to the sound of the honking taxis lined up behind me.

TWO

That night, instead of shooting Paul as he came through the front door, I allowed him one chance. I even waited until we were eating dinner to talk about what he'd been up to at lunchtime at the St Regis Hotel in Midtown.

Maybe there was some logical explanation. I couldn't imagine what it would be, but in the words of a bumper sticker I once saw, *Miracles Happen, Too*.

'So, Paul,' I said as casually as the liquid nitrogen pumping through my veins allowed me. 'What did you do for lunch today?'

That got his attention. Even though I had my head down as I nearly sawed through the plate under my food, I felt his head bob up, his eyes lift, as he looked at me.

Then, after an extended guilty pause, he looked back down at his plate.

'Had a sandwich at my desk,' he mumbled. 'The usual. You know me, Lauren.'

Paul lied – right to my face.

My dropped knife banged off my plate like a gong. The darkest paranoid possibilities flooded through me. Crazy stuff that wasn't really like me.

Maybe his job wasn't even real, I thought. Maybe he'd had a

letterhead made up, and from day one he'd been betraying me when he went downtown every day. How well did I really know his co-workers? Maybe they were actors hired to show up whenever I was planning to come by.

'Why do you ask?' Paul finally said, ever so casually. That hurt. Almost as much as seeing him with the stunning blonde in Manhattan.

Almost.

I don't know how I managed to smile at him, with the cat-five hurricane roaring through me, but somehow I managed to pull the tight muscles of my cheeks upward.

'Just making conversation,' I said. 'Just talking to my husband over dinner.'

PART ONE

THE QUICKIE

Chapter One

There was heavy traffic on the Major Deegan south, and more on the approach to the Triborough that night, that crazy, crazy night.

I couldn't decide which was making my eye twitch more as we crawled across the span – the horns from the cars logjammed in both directions around us, or the ones honking from our driver's Spanish music station.

I was heading to Virginia for a job-sponsored seminar.

Paul was going to apply some face time to one of his firm's biggest clients in Boston.

The only trip we modern, professional, go-getting Stillwells were going to share this week was the ride to LaGuardia Airport.

At least I had one of the great views of Manhattan outside my window. The Big Apple seemed even more majestic than usual with its glass-and-steel towers glowing against the approaching black thunderheads of a storm.

Gazing out, I remembered the cute apartment Paul and I once had on the Upper West Side. Saturdays at the Guggenheim or MOMA; the cheap hole-in-the-wall French bistro in NoHo; cold chardonnay in the 'backyard,' our fourth-floor studio's fire escape. All the romantic things we did before we got married, when our lives had been unpredictable and fun.

'Paul,' I said urgently, almost mournfully. *'Paul?'*

If Paul had been a 'guy guy,' I might have been tempted to chalk up what was happening between us to the inevitable. You grow a little bit older, maybe more cynical, and the honeymoon finally ends. But Paul and me? We'd been different.

We'd been one of those sickening, best-friend married couples. The let's-die-at-the-exact-same-moment Romeo-and-Juliet soul mates. Paul and I had been *so* much in love – and that's not just selective memory talking. That was us.

We'd met in freshman year at Fordham Law. We were in the same study and social group but hadn't really talked. I'd noticed Paul because he was very handsome. He was a few years older than most of us, a little more studious, more serious. I actually couldn't believe it when he agreed to head down to Cancún for spring break with the gang.

On the night before our flight home, I got into a fight with my boyfriend at the time and accidentally fell through one of the hotel's glass doors, cutting my arm. While my supposed boyfriend announced he 'just couldn't deal with it,' Paul arrived out of nowhere and took over.

He took me to the hospital and stayed at my bedside. This, while everyone else promptly hopped on the flight home to avoid missing any classes.

As Paul walked through the doorway of my Mexican hospital room with our breakfast of milkshakes and magazines, I was reminded of how cute he was, how deep blue his eyes were, and that he had fantastic dimples and a killer smile.

Dimples and milkshakes, and my heart.

What had happened since then? I wasn't entirely sure. I guess we'd fallen into the rut of a lot of modern marriages. Neck-deep into our two demanding, separate careers, we'd become so adept at meeting our individual needs and wants that we'd forgotten the point: that we were supposed to be putting each other first.

I still hadn't confronted Paul about the blonde woman I'd seen him with in Manhattan. Maybe that was because I wasn't ready to have it out with him once and for all. And, of course, I didn't know for sure if he was having an affair. Maybe I was afraid about the end of *us*. Paul had loved me; I know he had. And I had loved Paul with everything I had in me.

Maybe I still did. *Maybe.*

'Paul,' I called again.

Across the seat of the taxi, he turned at the sound of my voice. I felt like he was noticing me for the first time in weeks. An apologetic, almost sad expression formed on his face. His mouth started to open.

Then his blasted cell phone trilled. I remembered setting his ring tone to 'Tainted Love' as a prank. Ironically, a silly song we'd once danced to drunk and happy had turned out to aptly describe our marriage.

Glaring at the phone, I seriously considered snatching it from his hand and flinging it out the window through the bridge cables into the East River.

A familiar glaze came across Paul's eyes after he glanced down at the number.

'I have to take this,' he said, thumbing open the phone.

I don't, Paul, I thought as Manhattan slid away from us through the coiled steel.

This was it, I thought. The final straw. He'd wrecked everything between us, hadn't he?

And sitting there in that cab, I figured out the exact point when you call it quits.

When you can't even share a sunset together.

Chapter Two

Ominous thunder cracked in the distance as we pulled off the Grand Central Parkway into the airport. The late-summer sky was graying rapidly, bad weather was approaching with speed.

Paul was jabbering something about book values as we pulled up to my stop at the Continental terminal. I didn't expect him to do something as effort-filled as kiss me good-bye. When Paul had his low 'business voice' going on the phone, a bomb couldn't make him stop.

I reached quickly for the door when the driver switched the radio from the Spanish station to the financial news. If I didn't escape, I feared the insectile buzz of investo-speak in stereo was going to make me scream.

Until my throat bled.

Until I lost consciousness.

Paul waved from the back window without looking at me as the cab pulled away.

I was tempted to wave back with one finger as I rolled my suitcase through the sliding doors. But I didn't wave at all.

A few minutes later, I sat in the bar, waiting for my flight to be called, thinking very heavy thoughts. I took out the ticket as I sipped my cosmopolitan.

From the overhead speakers, a Muzak version of The Clash's 'Should I Stay or Should I Go?' was playing. How do you like that? The folks at Muzak had discovered my childhood.

It was good that I was feeling so manic and upbeat, because normally that realization might make me feel old and depressed.

I tapped the ticket against my lip, then very dramatically tore it in half before I finished my drink in one shot.

Next, I used the bar napkin to dry the tears in my eyes.

I was going to move on to Plan B.

It was going to be trouble, for sure. Big troubles, no bubbles.

I didn't care. Paul had ignored me too many times.

I made the phone call that I'd been putting off.

Then I rolled my suitcase back outside, climbed into the rear of the next available taxi, and gave the driver my home address.

The first drops of rain hit the windows as we pulled out, and I suddenly envisioned something huge slipping under dark water and beginning to slide, something monumental, slowly, irretrievably sinking. Down, down, down.

Or maybe not – just maybe, I was heading up for the first time in a long while.

Chapter Three

It was full-out pouring by the time I stepped back into my dark, empty house. I felt a little better when I switched my wet business suit for my old Amherst gym shirt and a pair of favorite jeans.

And a lot better when I put Stevie Ray Vaughan on the stereo to keep me company.

I decided to leave the lights off and crack open a dusty case of calla-lily-scented candles from the front-hall closet.

Pretty soon, the house was looking like a church, or maybe a loopy Madonna video, given the way the drapes were blowing around. It inspired me to scroll my iPod down to her pop highness's 'Dress You Up' and to crank up the sound.

Twenty minutes later, the front doorbell rang and the baby lamb chops I'd ordered on the cab ride home arrived.

I took the small, precious brown-paper package from the FreshDirect delivery guy, went into the kitchen, and poured myself a glass of Santa Margherita as I chopped garlic and lemons. After I put the red potatoes on for the garlic mash, I set the table.

For two.

I took my Santa Margherita upstairs.

That's when I noticed the insistent red blink on my answering machine.

'Yeah, hi, Lauren. Dr Marcuse here. I was leaving the office and just wanted to let you know that your results haven't come back yet. I know you're waiting. I'll let you know first thing after we hear from the lab.'

As the machine clicked off, I pulled back my hair and gazed into the mirror at the faint wrinkles on my forehead and at the corners of my eyes.

I was three weeks late with my period. Which normally wouldn't be a concern.

Except that I was infertile.

The results that my ever-helpful gynecologist, Dr Marcuse, was referring to were from the blood work and ultrasound he'd urged me to get.

It was a race at that point. A neck-and-neck downhill heat.

Which would fail first? I thought, lifting my glass.

My marriage or my health?

'Thanks for checking in, Dr Marcuse,' I said to the machine. 'Your timing is impeccable.'

Chapter Four

At this point, my heart was starting to race. *Dinner for two – and neither of them was Paul.*

After I finished my glass of wine, I went downstairs and did the only sensible thing under the circumstances. I found the bottle and took it back upstairs with me.

After I had filled my third glass, I carried it and my wedding picture on to my bed.

I sat and drank, and stared at Paul.

At first, I'd been pretty resigned to Paul's change in behavior after his latest and most pressure-filled promotion at work. I definitely thought it was unhealthy for him to be so stressed out all the time, but I also knew that investment finance was what he did. It was what he was good at, he'd told me many times. How he defined himself.

So I let it slide. His distance from me. The way he'd suddenly begun to ignore me at meals, and in the bedroom. He needed every ounce of concentration and energy for the office. And it was temporary, I told myself. Once he got up to speed, he would ease back. Or, at the very least, he would fail. I'd lick his wounds, and we'd be back to normal. I'd get to see those dimples again, that smile. We'd be back to being best friends.

I opened the night-table drawer and took out my charm bracelet.

On my first birthday after we were married, Paul had bought it for me from, of all places, the pre-teen store Limited Too. So far I had six charms, the first, and my favorite, being a rhinestone heart 'for his love,' he'd said.

I don't know why, but every year, each chintzy, puppy-love charm meant a million times more to me than the meal in the fancy restaurant he always took me to.

This year, Paul had gotten us into Per Se, the new white-hot spot in the Time Warner Center. But even after the crème brûlée, there was no gift.

He'd forgotten to get me a charm for the bracelet. Forgotten, or decided not to.

That had been the first sign of real trouble.

The Times Square neon billboard for trouble came in the form of the twenty-something blonde outside his office on Pearl Street – the one he'd taken into the St Regis.

The one Paul had lied to my face about.

Chapter Five

I was downstairs in the kitchen, laying the pink chops down into sizzling butter, when there was a hard rap on the window of the back door. The butterflies swirling in my stomach surged, changed formation. I looked at the clock on the microwave.

Eleven on the dot.

Here it was, *here he was,* I thought, dabbing the sweat from my forehead with a kitchen towel as I crossed to the door. It was actually happening.

Right here.

Right now.

I took a deep, deep breath and slipped open the dead bolt.

'Hi, Lauren.'

'Hi back at you. You look nice. Great.'

'For somebody who's soaking wet, right?'

The rain that swung in with the door spattered a constellation of dark, wet stars on the kitchen's pale stone tile.

And then he stepped in. Quite the entrance, I might add.

His tapered six-two frame seemed to fill the room. In the candlelight, I could see that his dark hair was freshly cut, the color of wet white sand where it was shaved close to his skull.

Wind roared in, and the scent of him, cologne and rain and

leather from the motorcycle jacket he wore, hit me head-on.

Oprah has probably devoted a couple of hours to how you get to this point, I thought as I struggled for something to say. Harmless workplace flirting that leads to infatuation that leads to a furtive friendship that leads to . . . I still wasn't sure what to call this.

I knew some married female co-workers who took part in harmless flirting, but I'd always put up a wall when I was dealing with men professionally, especially the handsome, funny ones like Scott. It just didn't feel right, going there.

But Scott had gotten over my wall somehow, gotten inside my defenses. Maybe it was the fact that, for all his size and good looks, there was an innocence about him. Or maybe it was how he was almost formal with me. Old-fashioned in the best sense of the word. Or how his presence in my life seemed to have increased in perfect ratio to Paul's pulling away.

And as if that weren't enough, there was something nicely mysterious about him, something subtle under the surface that pulled at me.

'So, you're actually here,' Scott said, breaking the silence between us. 'Wait, I almost forgot.'

For the first time, I noticed the wet, tattered brown bag he was holding. He blushed as he took a little stuffed animal out of it. It was a Beanie Baby, one I'd never seen before, a little tan puppy. I looked at the name tag, 'Badges.' Then I looked at the birthdate, *December 1*.

I put a hand to my open mouth.

My birthday.

I'd been looking for one with my birthday only for ever. Scott knew, and he had found it.

I looked at the puppy. Then I remembered how Paul had forgotten the charm for my bracelet. That's when I felt something break like thin ice inside me, and I was crying.

'Lauren, no,' Scott said, panicked. He raised his arms to embrace me, then stopped as if he'd run into some invisible wall.

'Listen,' he said. 'The last thing in the world I want to do is hurt you. This is all too much. I can see that now. I . . . I'll just go, okay? I'll see you tomorrow as usual. I'll bring the Box o' Joe, you bring the cinnamon Munchkins, and this never happened. Okay?'

Then my back door opened again, and Scott was gone into the night.

Chapter Six

I listened to the meat sizzle rather melodramatically as I wiped my eyes with a dish towel. What was I doing? Was I crazy? Scott was right. What the hell had I been thinking? I stood there dumbly staring at the puddles he'd made on the floor seconds ago.

Then, the next thing I knew, I turned off the stove, grabbed my handbag, threw the door open, and ran outside in the dark.

He was getting on his motorcycle half a block away when I caught up to him, completely drenched now myself.

A light went on in a neighbor's house. Mrs Waters was just about the biggest gossip on our block. What would she say if she saw me? Scott noticed me looking up at the window nervously.

'Here,' he said, handing me his helmet. 'Don't overthink this, Lauren. Just do it. Get on.'

I put the helmet on and took another, even stronger hit of Scott's scent as he started up his red Ducati racing bike. It sounded like something detonating.

'Come on,' he yelled, offering his hand. 'Quick!'

'Isn't it dangerous to ride in the rain?' I asked.

'Outrageously,' he said, grinning irresistibly as he gunned the throttle.

I put out my hand, and the next second I was climbing on behind Scott and wrapping my arms around his sides.

I had just enough time to tuck my head between his shoulder blades before we screamed up the hill of my cul-de-sac like a bottle rocket.

Chapter Seven

It's possible I left claw marks on Scott's leather jacket while I hung on for dear life. My stomach bottomed out whenever we hit a dip and then seemed to bang off the roof of my skull when we topped rises. The rain-slicked world appeared to melt away as we hurtled past.

I cursed myself for not drawing up a living will when the bike's back tire fishtailed on to the entrance to the Saw Mill River Parkway. Then Scott let the bike run loose!

The next time I breathed and looked up, we were pulling off the Henry Hudson Parkway into Riverdale, an upscale neighborhood in the Bronx.

We came roaring down a hill and only slowed as we turned on to a street lined with dark, gated mansions. In a flash of lightning I saw the wide silver chasm of the Hudson close below us, the stark, shattered face of the New Jersey Palisades directly across the water.

'C'mon, Lauren,' Scott said, suddenly stopping the bike and hopping off. He waved for me to follow him as he started walking up the cobblestone driveway of a colonial about the size of a Home Depot.

'You live here?' I called to him after I removed his helmet.

'Kinda,' Scott called back, waving some more.

'Kinda?'

I followed him into a free-standing three-car garage that was almost as big as my house. Inside, there was a Porsche, a Bentley, and a Ferrari the same color as Scott's bike.

'Those aren't yours!' I said in shock.

'I wish,' Scott said, climbing a set of stairs. 'They're more like my roommate's. I'm just house-sitting for this friend of mine. C'mon, I'll get us towels.'

I walked behind him into a small loft-style apartment above the garage. He popped open a couple of Budweisers and put on a Motown CD before he went into the bathroom. In the massive bay window, the storm-racked Hudson was framed like a billboard.

After Scott tossed me a fluffy towel that smelled of lemon, he stood on the bathroom threshold, just staring at me. Like I was beautiful or something.

It was the same way I'd caught him looking at me down a corridor or in the parking lot or stairwell at work.

A kind of pleading in his almond-shaped brown eyes.

For the first time I allowed myself to stare back. I took a sip of cold beer.

Then my beer dropped from my hand as I suddenly realized why I was so attracted to him. It was crazy, really. When I was in high school, I met a boy on summer vacation at Spring Lake on the Jersey Shore. He was in charge of the bike-rental place by the boardwalk, and let me tell you, Lance Armstrong didn't put in as much roadwork that summer as I did.

Then one Friday night, the most momentous Friday in my life up to that point, he invited me to my first beach party.

I guess every life has at least one golden moment, right? A period of time when the glory of the world and your place in it briefly and magically align.

That beach party was mine.

There I was. My first honest-to-God beer buzz, the ocean crashing in the background, the evening sky the color of turquoise, as this perfect older boy reached out across the sand and without a word took my hand in his. I was sixteen years old. My braces were off, my burn had finally started to turn to brown, and I had a sense of infinite possibilities and a stomach you could bounce a quarter off.

That's who Scott reminded me of, I realized, staring at the light in his eyes – Mike, the Jersey Shore bike boy, come to take me back to the endless beach party, where there were no high-stress jobs, no biopsies, and no cheating husbands with attractive blondes on their arm.

And I guess, right then, what I wanted more than anything, at the most confusing, shitty time of my entire life, was to go back there with him. And be that sixteen-year-old girl again.

Scott was down on his knees, wiping up the beer spill. I took a breath, reached out, and brushed my hand over his head. 'You're sweet,' I whispered.

Scott stood up and held my face in his hands. 'No, you're the one who's sweet. And you're the most beautiful woman I know, Lauren. Kiss me. *Please.*'

Chapter Eight

Paul and I had once had a sweet sex life. In the early days, we were inseparable. On the way down to our third honeymoon, in Barbados, we even became full-fledged members of the Mile High Club.

But being with Scott?

It was life-threatening.

For the better part of an hour, we just kissed and caressed and fondled, my breath and heart rate accelerating in dangerous increments with each button release, every tug of my clothes. When Scott eventually pulled up my shirt and pressed his face to my stomach, I almost bit through my lower lip.

Then he popped the top button of my jeans. From my throat came a sound that wasn't even close to human. I was in danger of passing out, and loving it.

We staggered from room to room, shedding each other's clothes. We clinched, straining against each other, desperate for breath. I had been needing this for so long, especially the touches, the caresses, maybe just the attention.

How we actually ended up in his bed, I can't quite remember. Somewhere near the end, I recall, lightning struck so close in the backyard that the window rattled in its frame in time to the headboard.

Maybe God was trying to tell me something.

But I don't think we could have stopped if the roof of the house had been ripped away.

Afterward I lay there on the comforter, shuddering like a trauma victim, sweat covering my cheeks and neck, my lungs stinging. The wind howled against the windowpane as Scott rolled his searing body off mine. 'Jeez, Lauren. My God, you're great.'

I was afraid he might stand up and offer to take me home then. I was happily relieved when he spooned in beside me, resting his chin on my shoulder. As we cuddled in the dark, all I could think about were those eyes of his, those gentle, almost auburn-colored eyes, as he finger-combed my hair.

'I think I need a shower,' he said finally. His long, muscular legs seemed to wobble when he stood. 'Check that out. I need an IV.'

'You could get one at the emergency room when you drop me off,' I said, smiling.

I had just enough energy to prop my head on a pillow as Scott walked to the bathroom. I could see him in the mirror when he turned on the light. He was beautiful. Honest to God he was.

His bunched muscles dug into his sides and his tanned back. He looked like something off a Calvin Klein billboard.

It had been . . . perfect, I thought. Better than I had had any reason to expect. Undeniably hot, but also sweet. I hadn't thought Scott would be so affectionate, that we would connect emotionally as well as physically.

I'd needed to have this happen, I realized. To feel hot and then warm. To laugh. To be held close by someone who liked me and who thought I was special.

And I refuse to feel guilty, I thought, listening to another close explosion of thunder.

What's good for the goose is definitely good for the desperate housewife. Even if this never happened again – and maybe it wouldn't, shouldn't – it was worth it.

Chapter Nine

In the cramped dark of his Toyota Camry parked half a block north of the apartment over the garage, Paul Stillwell stared, mesmerized, as another flash of lightning illuminated Scott's shiny red motorcycle.

He'd actually seen the Ducati in the centerfold of the FYI section of *Fortune* magazine once, one of those impossibly expensive fantasy boy toys. Something a movie star or the devil-may-care heir to a European shipping conglomerate might ride.

And happy assholes like Scott, Paul thought, staring at its fighter-jet contours, red and slick as lip gloss in the shimmer of light.

His throat tightened as he tore his eyes away and went back to scrolling through the pictures file on his Verizon cell.

He stopped at the shot of Scott that he'd taken when he followed Scott home from work the week before. In the photograph, Scott was astride the Italian bike at a stoplight, his full-face helmet perched back on his forehead. Lean, powerful, and as cocky as the expensive machine between his legs.

Paul closed the cell and stared out through the rain at the light in the garage's upstairs window.

Then he leaned back and lifted the Ping 3 iron from the floor of the backseat. The golf club had good heft and balance.

It was a drastic solution, he knew, staring at the heavy, fist-size metal club's face. But what choice did you have when a man invaded your house and took what was yours?

Everything was in jeopardy now, he reminded himself. Everything he'd worked for was in danger of slipping through his fingers.

Maybe he should have done something sooner. Headed things off before it came to this. But maybes and should haves and if onlys were beside the point now, weren't they? One question remained: Would he allow this bullshit to continue or would he not?

No, Paul thought, cutting the ignition. There's only one way to end this.

The rain rattled on the roof of the Camry. He pocketed his cell phone and took a deep breath. With slow, almost ceremonial deliberation, he wrapped his black-gloved hand around the grip of the perfectly weighted club.

The extreme hard way, he thought, and he opened the car door and stepped out into the driving rain.

Chapter Ten

'So, what now?' Scott said, pulling his jacket on over his bare chest as he came out of the shower.

'Surprise me,' I said. 'I like surprises. I love surprises.'

Scott bent over and took my left wrist. My vision went double as he softly kissed my pulse point.

'How was that?' he said, smiling.

'Nice start,' I said when my lung function finally returned.

'You stay here while I spin by the all-night market. I'm out of fresh basil and olive oil,' Scott said, standing. 'You don't mind if I whip us up a late dinner, do you? I have some great veal cutlets I got on Arthur Avenue yesterday. I'll make you my mom's sauce. It's better than Rao's.'

Mind! I thought, envisioning Scott in an apron. *A man actually cooking for me?*

'I could probably suffer through it,' I said after I finished swallowing really hard.

Scott was opening the door, when he suddenly stopped and turned, staring back at me.

'What?' I said. 'Changed your mind about cooking?'

'I . . . ,' he said, 'I guess I'm just glad we did this tonight,

Lauren. I wasn't sure if you would go through with it. I'm glad you did. I'm really glad we did.'

Wow, I thought, smiling as he closed the door. I looked out at the storm-racked Hudson. Scott probably had the right idea, didn't he? Live for the moment. Forever young. Carefree. Maybe I could get used to this.

I glanced at my watch. Just after one. Where was I supposed to be now? In bed in some cramped Virginia Marriott.

Sorry, Paul, I thought. But remember, you started this.

I decided to call him and get it over with. It was as good a time as any to go through the motions. Paul liked charades, didn't he?

I could play at that game too, I thought as I rolled off the bed, looking for my bag and my cell phone.

Chapter Eleven

There's my boy, Paul thought as Scott Thayer threw open the side door of the garage. *Hey there, Scotty.*

Dressed all in black and crouched in the shadows along the ivy-covered wall beside Scott's parked motorcycle, Paul knew he wouldn't be seen. Besides, it was raining like hell.

Paul hefted the golf club as Scott came across the driveway and entered the dark street. Time to show this son of a bitch the error of his ways.

Scott was ten feet away. Five.

Then suddenly, inexplicably, horribly, there was music blaring from somewhere. From him! From Paul's jacket pocket! His cell phone was going off!

No! Paul thought, reaching down to silence the stupid 'Tainted Love' ring tone. Why the hell hadn't he left his cell in the car?

He was fumbling to turn it off with his free hand when Scott Thayer crashed into him at a run. Paul's breath left him as he was knocked backward on to the muddy ground.

He looked up, meeting Scott's wide eyes.

'You!' Scott said in shock. The golf club disappeared out of Paul's hand as Scott kick-smashed his motorcycle boot into Paul's fingers. Then Scott lifted Paul off his feet and threw him into the air. Paul cried out as his back struck something painfully hard. It was the Ducati. He and the bike went over in a pitiful heap.

'If I didn't know any better, I'd think you were planning on doing me some harm tonight, Mr Stillwell,' Scott said, not even breathing heavily. He lifted the fallen club as he slowly approached.

'Something like this could really hurt somebody,' Scott said, waving the 3 iron at him like a chiding finger. 'Here, let me show you.'

Chapter Twelve

I stood there, frozen, my nose millimeters from the rain-streaked glass as I looked out at the private street in front of the garage.

I couldn't believe what I was seeing. *This isn't happening,* I thought. *It can't be happening.*

Paul was here?

And he and Scott were fighting in the street! Really going at each other.

I'd gone to the window when I heard the crash of the motorcycle. Then I found myself immobile, unable to do anything but stand and stare at the unbelievable scene.

Of course Paul was here, I thought, reeling. What an idiot I'd been! Scott and I hadn't been discreet. We'd sent e-mails back and forth. I'd actually put Scott's number in my cell phone. Paul had simply started keeping tabs.

Guilt rattled through me. And fear.

What had I been thinking?

For weeks I'd tortured myself, imagining Paul with his blonde lover. Night after night, I'd envisioned them making love in their St Regis suite. I was wallowing in the pain that only a spouse who realizes they're being cheated on feels. Pathetic.

But imagining was one thing.

Doing the same thing as revenge was another.

I'd just had a quickie for Christ's sake!

I watched, helpless, as Paul and Scott crashed into each other. Then the fight moved out of my line of sight, blocked by the vine-covered wall across the street. The two of them became just shadows. Violent ones that grappled and walloped and kicked at each other. What was happening now?

I couldn't think of what to do. Call out? Try to stop them?

And I was only looking at the preamble. It would be even worse when the fight was over and Paul came inside. When I had to face him.

I didn't know how I was going to do that.

Suddenly, there was a tremendous crack, like a well-hit base-ball, and I didn't have to think about it anymore.

Both shadows stopped moving.

Then one dropped. He actually bounced off the ground before he lay completely still.

Who was hurt? Who was down? I wondered with a kind of dumbstruck curiosity. Then the scariest question of all occurred to me. One that took my breath away as it nicked through my heart like a cold razor.

Who did I want it to be?

Chapter Thirteen

For a heart-punishing minute, everything was dead still. The shadow figures outside. My breathing. Even the rain seemed to have stopped. The silence was so absolute it seemed to ring.

Then from out of it came a far-off thump. Then another thump. *Thump, thump, thump.* I thought it might be the sound of my heart amplified by terror until a silvery glow cut through the darkness.

The unmistakable throbbing assault of cranked-up rap music reached my eardrums as a tricked-out Acura pulled on to the street and then into a driveway at the far end of the block.

For the briefest moment, powerful xenon headlights lit the opposite side of the street, revealing the unforgettable scene in its startling entirety.

It only took a millisecond, but that was more than enough time for the image to be burned forever into my memory.

The standing shadow was definitely Paul. He was breathing heavily, holding Scott's motorcycle helmet in his hand like a club.

Scott lay at his feet, a golf club near his hand, a black halo of blood beneath his head.

This is what happens when you cheat, a voice whispered in my ear.

This is what you get.

Then, at that moment, I did the most constructive thing I could think of. I dropped away from the window and hid my face in my hands.

Scott was down, not moving.

Because of me.

I was still in full-body lockdown, fumbling with these new, numbing realities, when another thought occurred to me.

Was Paul crazy enough to come after me too?

Overcome with the need to see where Paul was now, I went back to the window.

What the hell?

Parked directly behind Scott's fallen motorcycle, in the dome of light, was Paul's car. I watched in horror as Paul tossed Scott on to the backseat. It seemed like Scott's head banged against the door frame, and I heard him groan.

What did Paul think he was doing?

Finally, I rushed down the stairs of the apartment. I couldn't let this continue. I went through CPR procedure in my head. Mouth-to-mouth. I was almost at the door when I suddenly realized I didn't have any clothes on. I hurried back upstairs.

I had my T-shirt on and was fumbling with my jeans when I heard the thunk of a car door closing, and then the sound of tires spinning.

I rushed to the window again.

I looked out just in time to see Paul's car speeding away.

My chest burning, my head spinning, I had one more question for Paul as I watched the car's red running lights disappear into the darkness.

Where the hell are you going with Scott?

Chapter Fourteen

It took me a full two minutes to realize what must have happened. Two mind-and-body-numbing minutes of leaning my head against the cold, rain-streaked glass. I smiled when the sweet logic of it suddenly struck me. For the first time that night, my heart slowed slightly and approached a semi-human rate.

Paul must have taken Scott to the hospital.

Of course he had. Paul had come to his senses. Sure, he'd lost it for a few minutes. Who wouldn't, catching up with the man who was sleeping with his wife? But after Scott had gone down, Paul finally snapped out of it.

They had to be pulling up to the emergency room of the closest hospital right now.

I called a taxi and arrived back home in Yonkers an excruciating forty minutes later. I threw open the door and stood there, staring at the microwave clock in the silent house.

Where was Paul? Shouldn't he be back by now? What was happening?

I decided Paul had taken Scott to Lawrence Hospital about ten minutes away from Scott's apartment. But now over an hour had passed. There was no word. Had something even more terrible happened? Maybe Paul had been arrested.

I checked the answering machine upstairs, but other than my gynecologist's dispatch on my failing health, it was empty. After another five minutes, spent staring at the empty street, I seriously considered giving Paul a call on his cell to see what was going on. The problem was, I didn't know exactly how to phrase things.

Hi, Paul? Yeah, it's me, Lauren. How's the guy I was screwing behind your back coming along? Is he going to be okay?

I needed to find out what was going on firsthand, I finally decided. But waiting around like this was making me insane.

It was time to face the music.

I needed to go to the hospital. I grabbed my gun, tossed it in my handbag, and ran out the door.

Chapter Fifteen

Thank God for ABS, I thought as I came centimeters from rear-ending with my Mini Cooper the shiny ambulance parked in front of the Lawrence Hospital ER.

'Where's the beating victim?' I called to the polished-looking red-haired nurse behind the Plexiglas at the triage desk.

'Oh my God! You were beaten?' she said, spilling the *People* magazine out of her lap as she stood.

I looked around the waiting room. It was empty. Stranger than that, it was clean. Calming classical music serenaded from the overhead speakers. Bronxville, Yonkers' extremely wealthy neighbor to the east, was one of the most upscale suburbs in Westchester, I remembered. Lawrence Hospital did lacrosse injuries, and the occasional Oxy overdose or debutante who'd fallen off her horse.

I rolled my eyes as I headed back to the parking lot.

A bloody John Doe couldn't have been left at Lawrence Hospital's doorstep, I realized, because the entire Bronxville police force wasn't here. So, where could Paul have taken Scott?

I racked my brain for the next-nearest hospital.

Our Lady of Mercy Medical Center, to the south on the Bronx River Parkway, I decided, as I peeled out into the wet street once again.

Back down in the real Bronx. The one without the *ville*.

After hammering it down the parkway for ten minutes, I noticed that the center-doored colonials that bookended the parkway had been replaced by less quaint, gritty tenements. Steve McQueen would have been proud of the fishtailing stop I made before I ran into the ER entrance of Our Lady of Mercy on East 233rd Street.

I heard vociferous complaints as I cut to the head of the long triage line in the packed, grimy waiting room.

'Have you had any anonymous beating victims in the last hour?' I yelled to the first nurse I could find.

She replaced the bloody dish towel over the barbecue fork stuck in the hand of the Hispanic woman beside her before she looked up.

'He's in three,' she said, annoyed. 'Who the hell are you?'

More shouts followed me as I rushed through the open door behind her. I found number 3 and ripped back the green plastic curtain around it.

'Ever hear a knockin', bitch?' a near-naked black kid asked me in a malevolent tone as he attempted to cover himself with the hand not cuffed to the bed rail. A big white bandage was wrapped around his head, and a big white uniformed cop was sitting by his feet.

I felt something shift ominously in my stomach.

If Scott wasn't here, I thought . . .

Then where the hell was he? And where was Paul?

'Yo, Earth to lady,' the Bronx uniform said to me with a snap of his fingers. 'What's up?'

I was fumbling for a lie when I heard two loud beeps cut from the static of his radio.

He ignored me for a moment as he turned it up. The words were too garbled for me to catch everything, but I heard something about a white male victim, along with an address.

St James Park. Fordham Road and Jerome Avenue.

White male? I thought. No way. Impossible. Had to be a co-incidence.

I closed my gaping mouth as the cop directed his suspicious stare back at me.

'So you're saying this isn't where I hand in my urine sample?' I said, backing away.

Minutes later I was flooring it, heading south down the Bronx River Parkway. I'd just swing by, I told myself as I rocketed off at the Fordham Road exit. No biggie. It was almost stupid, really. Because Scott couldn't be at some Bronx crime scene. Because he was right now at a hospital, being treated for some cuts and bruises. Minor cuts and bruises, I reminded myself.

I rolled west up Fordham Road. I passed under a sign above a broken streetlight that proclaimed, 'The Bronx Is Back.' Where had it been? I thought, staring at the steel-shuttered Spanish clothing stores interrupted by the occasional Popeye's Fried Chicken or Taco Bell.

I made a hard right on to Jerome Avenue.

And slammed on the Mini's brakes with both feet.

Chapter Sixteen

I'd never seen so many NYPD cop cars in one place. They were
on the sidewalk, under the elevated track, parked like a wagon
train in St James, a block-square concrete park. Every one of their
blue and red and yellow lights was flying full throttle. There was
so much yellow crime-scene tape, it looked like Christo had
decided to do a yellow-and-black installation in the Bronx.

Keep going, a voice whispered in the back of my mind. Some
ER doctor is sewing Scott's stitches right at this very moment.
Or, who knew? Maybe Paul had already dropped him back at his
place.

*Get out of this wretched place right now. You'll get into trouble,
big trouble, if you stay here.*

But I couldn't go. I needed to be sure. I needed to act respon-
sibly. Starting right now.

I rolled directly toward the commotion.

The thin, silver-haired cop directing traffic around the light
show gave me a look of eye-boggled shock as I stopped my car
almost on top of him.

He was reaching for his cuffs when I opened the door and all
but fell out of my car. When I went into my handbag, he changed
his mind and went for his Glock instead.

But then I took it out.

Took out my badge.

The gold badge I'd been given when the NYPD promoted me to detective.

'Jesus,' the relieved-looking uniform said as he lifted the yellow tape behind him and beckoned me under.

'Why didn't you just say you were on The Job?'

Chapter Seventeen

I'd been a cop for seven years, the last year and a half as a Detective First Grade on the Bronx Homicide Task Force. Which made my co-worker Scott Thayer a cop too. Detective Third Grade with Bronx Narcotics.

What can I say?

Office affairs happen in the NYPD too.

I dodged under the yellow tape and walked toward the blinding white floodlights the Crime Scene Unit had set up at the center of the park. Maybe it was just my frazzled state, but I was all too familiar with crime scenes and I'd never seen one quite so frantic, or one filled with so many pissed-off cops. What the hell was going on?

I walked past rusted monkey bars and a graffiti-covered wall for handball.

I stopped in the darkness just beyond where the lights blazed down on a fountain so old and exhaust-stained that its granite looked black.

A blue plastic tarp around its ornate base was half floating in the water, covering something. What was under the blue tarp?

I had a feeling it wasn't some new artwork about to be unveiled up here in the Bronx.

I almost jumped as a hand, large and warm, palmed the standing hairs at the back of my neck.

'What are you doing here, Lauren?' Detective Mike Ortiz said with his ever-serene half-smile.

Mike, my partner for the past year, was in his midforties and about as laid-back as he was large. He was constantly being mistaken for The Rock, so I guess that made him confident enough to be laid-back, or any other way he wanted to be.

'Aren't you supposed to be down in Quantico, handing out, I mean, picking up, tips at the FBI Academy?' Mike asked.

My seminar in Virginia was with the FBI's Behavioral Science Unit, an NYPD-sponsored brushup on the latest investigative techniques.

'Missed my flight,' I managed to get out. 'I'll get an early one tomorrow.'

Mike clucked his tongue as he nudged me forward into the spotlight beside the fountain. 'I have a funny feeling you're going to wish you'd made that plane,' he said.

My partner tossed me a pair of rubber boots and gloves as we got to the fountain's scrolled stone rim. I slowly pulled them on and then swung myself over the edge and down into the water.

The icy rainwater went to about mid-shin.

I kept my questionable balance and motion forward by concentrating on the glitter of the police lights inside the rain pocks. They looked like tiny fireworks, I thought as I waded closer to the tarp. Little red and blue blossoms of light. Kind of unreal, like everything else tonight.

This was stupid, I thought with conviction as I sloshed even closer.

Because there was a drug dealer under the tarp. Or just another junkie. People like me always ended up doing a meet-and-greet with them, just like tonight.

Then I was finally beside the blue tarp under the hot, unforgiving glare of the portable light carts. No more delaying. I couldn't have turned back now if I'd wanted to. Mike Ortiz was right behind me. 'Do the honors, Lauren,' he said.

I held my breath.

And tugged the sheet away.

Chapter Eighteen

Jesus God, help me, I thought.

My next thought was even weirder.

When I was seven years old, I caught a men's softball game line drive right in my chest. It was at our Bronx Irish neighborhood's annual NYPD vs FDNY barbecue, and it happened as I was on the Finest first-base line, cheering on my patrol sergeant dad, who was on the mound, pitching. I don't remember the ball hitting me, don't remember a thing about it. They said that my heart actually stopped. My father had to give me CPR until they defibrillated me. I don't remember any light at the end of a tunnel or any sweet-faced guardian angels beckoning me heavenward. Only pain and the silently moving mouths of the adults looking down at me, seen as if through an incredibly thick piece of glass.

I felt that exact same sense of disconnection as I looked down.

And saw warm brown eyes staring up at me through a foot of bloody rainwater.

I almost hugged Scott right there and then. Almost dropped right into the water beside him in all my clothes, wrapped my arms around him.

Except I was unable to move.

I remembered the first time we met, at the 48th Precinct under the Cross Bronx Expressway. I was working overtime in the Homicide squad room upstairs, and Scott was working OT out of Narcotics downstairs, when the soda machine in the muster room wouldn't take my dollar. He gave me one of his, and when I hit the button, two Diet Cokes dropped down.

'Don't worry,' Scott said, smiling. You could almost hear the click as our eyes met. 'I won't tell Internal Affairs.'

I swallowed as the rain fell around me now. I eyed the tiny circles it was making over Scott's dead eyes.

'One of the uniforms ID'd him. Name's Scott Thayer,' Mike said. 'He's a detective from Bronx Narcotics. One of us, Lauren. This is as bad as it gets. Somebody killed a cop.'

My hands went up to my leaking eyes. I contemplated ripping them out.

'He was beaten very badly,' my partner continued, sounding to me like he was speaking from somewhere out past Pluto.

I nodded. Tell me something I don't know, I thought.

Then Mike did.

'Beaten to a pulp,' he said, anger seeping into his voice. 'And then somebody shot him.'

Chapter Nineteen

S *hot him?*

'See the entry wound under his left jaw?' my partner said, pointing as he continued to talk in a soft, mournful way.

I stared, nodded. I couldn't believe that I'd missed it. It looked like a misplaced belly button. I shuddered as I suddenly remembered the feel of Scott's stubble on my stomach.

'And the corneas.'

I nodded. Death sometimes makes the corneas look blurry after a few hours. Scott's were clear, indicating that he'd died very recently.

'He's got an ankle holster, but the gun is missing,' Mike said. 'It's a small holster, so I'm not sure if it was his service weapon . . . or maybe a throw-down in case he got into a questionable shoot. Who knows what he was doing here? Anyway, better to be tried by twelve than carried out by six, right? But it looks like Scott missed his day in court. God help him.'

This was one reason not to get involved in an office romance, I thought as I stepped out of the fountain and collapsed back against the cold, wet edge a minute or so later.

My brain made itself semi-useful by locking on to one word as I sat there. It banged against my skull, ricocheting off the inside like a trapped bird looking for an escape.

Why?

Why? Why? Why?

Scott had been alive. I'd heard him moan when Paul put him in the car. I was a Homicide detective, a trained expert in these kinds of things. Scott had been alive.

Had been, I thought, alternating glances between the tarp and the ground under my feet. After a while, I noticed that it wasn't actually a tarp. It was a Neat Sheet.

I shook my head in disbelief. I remembered clearly the trip to Stop & Shop when I bought the picnic blanket for Paul to keep in the trunk of his car.

Paul, you idiot, I thought as tears sprang hot from my eyes.

You stupid, goddamn idiot.

'I know, Lauren,' Mike said as he sat down beside me. 'That might as well be you in there,' he said. 'Might as well be me. Imagine, everything he ever worked for. Everything he ever enjoyed. Ever planned.'

Mike shook his head grimly.

'Dumped into a Bronx fountain like so much garbage.'

For a moment I felt the immense weight of my guilt. The idea of owning up hovered over me like a waiting avalanche. All I needed to do was turn to my partner and spill my guts. Tell him everything. Commence the end of my life as I knew it.

But I just couldn't make the words come out. Not now, anyway. Was it some instinctual desire to protect Paul? To protect myself? I don't know, I sincerely don't.

But I didn't say anything to my partner and the moment passed.

I kept my thoughts to myself and shook as I cried.

Chapter Twenty

I was still wiping my eyes when a pair of clunky black shoes appeared in front of my rubber boots.

I tilted my head up and saw my boss, Lieutenant Pete Keane. Irish, fair-skinned, baby-faced, and near-skeletal. The overseer of the Bronx Homicide Task Force could have passed for an aging altar boy if not for the flat nail heads of his hard gray eyes.

'Lauren,' he said. 'Came in when you heard the bad news, huh? I'm really glad you did. Saves me a call. I want you to be the primary investigator on this. You and Mike'll be the perfect team. You're my go-to guys, right?'

I stared at Pete Keane. Things were happening at warp speed. I was hardly reconciled to the fact that Scott was dead, and now my boss wanted me to be in charge of the case?

I wondered suddenly if Keane had learned about our affair. Jesus. Maybe he suspected I knew something about Scott's death and was testing me. Was that it?

No, I thought. That was impossible. Nobody knew at work. Scott and I had gone to painstaking lengths to make sure of that. Besides, nothing except flirting and a few meals had even happened between us. Until tonight, of course.

Actually, it felt like just about every conceivable thing had happened between me and Scott tonight.

It was only that Pete Keane liked me for big cases, I realized after a paranoia-dissipating breath. There were detectives on our squad who were senior to me, but I, his 'lady lawyer cop,' as he liked to call me, was a perfectionist. I put my law school training to work in the Homicide squad. I went methodically by the book, was completely thorough, completely organized, and I had a very high success rate. Bronx assistant DAs practically fought to take my cases because they could just about read my reports aloud for their prosecutions.

In a big-daddy political-shit-storm case like this, it would be all about reports, I realized. The ones that would have to be sent up the chain of command on practically an hourly basis.

I wanted nothing more than to get the hell out of there. I needed time to think, to sift through the pieces of my blown-apart life.

I felt the knot in my stomach twist like a corkscrew. In the end, it all came down to my inability to come up with a plausible excuse for not taking the assignment. For the moment, words failed me.

'Whatever you want, Pete,' I found myself saying.

My boss nodded.

'Scott Thayer,' he said, shaking his head wearily. 'Goddamn twenty-nine years old. Unbelievable. You guys know him at all?'

Mike blew on his coffee, shook his head.

My boss turned to me.

'How about you, Lauren?' he said.

How could I deny Scott? I thought. Only hours before, he'd stared into my eyes as he stroked my hair in his bed. Now he was lying there cold on stone, the expression of pain on his face reserved only for those who die completely alone.

The number 4 train screeched past on the elevated track on Jerome Avenue behind us. The blue-white light of its sparks snapped against the dark faces of the surrounding tenements.

'The name sounds familiar, I think,' I lied as I peeled off a rubber glove.

My first lie, I thought, looking out at the sea of NYPD blue and the flashing firefight of emergency lights.

I had a feeling it wasn't going to be my last.

Chapter Twenty-one

'Give me what you got so far,' Keane said. 'Commissioner just got off the Whitestone. I need smoke to blow up his ass – and keep it coming. What's your initial read on the crime scene? Impressions – anything at all?'

'Massive lacerations and contusions to the face,' Mike said. 'And one bullet wound under the left jaw. Maybe more, but we're still waiting on the ME so we can roll him.'

'Caliber?'

'Medium. A .38 maybe,' Mike guessed with a shrug of his shoulders.

'Service weapon or badge anywhere?'

Mike shook his head grimly.

'First impression is that somebody threw Thayer an incredible beating, shot him, and then dumped him here. Somebody pretty perturbed.'

'You agree, Lauren?' my boss asked.

I nodded, cleared my throat.

'Looks like it,' I said.

'Why do you say "dumped him"?' Keane asked next. 'You pretty sure Thayer wasn't killed here?'

'Not much blood in the fountain. Plus, his clothes are covered in mud and grass stains,' Mike said. 'This park hasn't seen grass since the Iroquois Nation.'

'Do your canvass forthwith,' Keane said. 'Talk to the ME and crime-scene, then get your asses into Thayer's office and check out his caseload. See what was open, what he was doing. The other members of his Drug Enforcement Task Force are being called as we speak. Talk to them when they get in. Talk to everybody in the squad.'

Keane turned as a speeding four-car entourage arrived beneath the elevated track from the south. He gave me a fatherly pat on the back.

'They're probably going to try to give this to those prima donnas at Major Case, but I'm not going to let them do it. This happened in our house. Make me proud.'

Chapter Twenty-two

Make my boss proud? I thought numbly as Pete Keane walked away.

That was going to take some doing.

Wait a second, I thought. Where was Paul? I'd been so busy being angry at him, I hadn't even thought to check if he was okay. For the first time, I realized something chilling.

For all I knew, he could have been shot too! That actually made some sense to me.

I tried Paul's cell first. My stomach dropped as his voice mail picked up.

I had to see if he was okay.

'Damn,' I said, slapping my forehead with my phone as I looked up at my partner. 'You're not going to believe this, but I had terrible insomnia last night, so I was up baking, and I left something in the oven. I need to swing by my house, Mike. You think you could cover for me for about half an hour?'

'What?' Mike said, shaking his head. 'Biggest case of our lives and . . . What was it, anyway?'

'Brownies.'

'Okay, Betty Crocker,' Mike said with a dumbfounded shake of his head. 'I got you covered for now. We have to wait around for the ME, anyway. Anybody asks, I'll tell them you went to swing by Scott's office. But you better fly, Ms Primary Investigator. I don't think the LT is going to be too happy if you're not here when he gets back, even if you bring him a midnight snack.'

I did as I was instructed. My lead foot coupled with the portable cop light I kept in my Mini had me back at my house in about eight minutes flat.

But as I crested the top of our cul-de-sac and spotted Paul's car in the driveway and the light on in our bedroom, I eased off the gas. A wave of relief washed over me.

Paul was home, at least.

Chapter Twenty-three

The car gave me an idea. Finally, my brain was starting to function again. I killed my headlights along with my siren and dash light and cruised toward my house like I was about to commit a burglary. I needed to figure out as much as I could before I faced Paul. I parked three houses down the street and walked the rest of the way.

The Camry's doors were locked, but with the Slim Jim I retrieved from the trunk of my Mini, it was only a temporary setback. I paused at the driver-side door as the smell hit me. Pine cleaner and bleach. *Somebody had cleaned up a mess.* I shook off my emotions, took a breath, and clicked on my Mini Maglite.

A few drops of blood under the passenger-side rear floor mat were all that I could find.

It took me all of three minutes to find the bullet hole.

It was underneath the driver's headrest. It had gone in but it hadn't come out. I probed the hole with the blade of the Leatherman tool I always carried and heard it click against something hard. A few saws later, the mushroomed lead slug dropped out of the hole right into my hand.

I placed it in my handbag, closed my eyes, and pieced the situation together as best I could.

Paul must have been driving when Scott, lying on the back-seat, came to. Disoriented and fearing for his life, Scott probably drew his ankle gun and fired once at Paul. The first round had hit the headrest.

Paul might have turned then and struggled for the gun. Then it must have gone off again.

In Scott's jaw. *Jesus, God.*

I took a scalding breath of bleach before I continued my reasoning, such as it was.

After that, Paul must have panicked. Even in self-defense, he knew that a dead cop just wasn't going to go away. So he'd come up with a quick plan, the best he could do. Scott was a cop. Who kills cops? Drug dealers kill cops. So Paul had driven into the Bronx and didn't stop until he found a busy drug area. Then he dumped Scott, came back home, and cleaned the car.

I shook my head as tears welled in my eyes again. For about five minutes, I knelt over where Paul had killed Scott and wept until my eyes ached.

This wasn't fair. It wasn't right. One mistake in judgment and now three lives were totally wrecked. I finally wiped my tears and got out of the car and headed for my house. And Paul.

But first I made a little side trip.

Chapter Twenty-four

I am a Homicide detective, and a pretty good one, and I easily found Scott's gun and badge in our garden toolshed.

It takes a lot of work and cleaning materials to erase a crime scene. I didn't see any obvious evidence in our garbage can outside the garage, so I went to the next logical hiding place. On the other side of the shed door was one of the Stop & Shop bags we used for garbage. It was brimming with blood-pink paper towels.

And underneath the bag were Scott's badge and the gun Paul had used to kill him.

It was a short-barreled Colt .38 revolver, a Detective Special. It was special, all right. I used one of the paper towels to lift it. I tipped out the chamber and looked at the dark holes where two rounds were missing.

I carefully placed it back under the bag and then locked the shed. I was walking up the driveway to my front door when my cell vibrated.

I looked at the caller ID, then at my lit bedroom window. I pressed myself into the shadows beside the garage door.

It was Paul.

What did he want? Should I pick up and talk to him? Had he seen me? I wimped out and let my voice mail take it. I played his message back a few seconds later.

'Hi, Lauren. It's me. I'm at home. I ran into difficulties with my flight. I'll explain what happened later. Was there a problem with your flight too? I noticed that your car's not here. Are you at work? Give me a call when you get a chance, okay? I'm worried about you.'

Worried about *me*? I thought, staring up at my window. Why? *I* didn't kill anybody.

Could this get any more bizarre? At least he was all right, I finally thought, folding my phone closed.

Paul was all right physically, if not otherwise.

I was taking a deep breath by my porch stairs, preparing myself to finally go inside and face him, when my phone vibrated again.

But it wasn't Paul this time.

It was my partner. I headed back into the shadows by the garage before I picked up.

'Mike?'

'Time's up, Lauren,' he said. 'Keane's on the move. I won't be able to stall for you much longer. You have to get back here now.'

'On my way,' I said.

I looked up at my window again. What the hell was I waiting for? I thought. Why was I skulking around in the dark outside my own house? I needed to go in and talk to Paul. Get some crisis management in motion. Call a good lawyer. Be rational. Be an adult. Figure this thing out somehow.

It was just a matter of looking Paul in the eye and saying, 'Yes, I cheated on you. Yes, I made love to another man tonight, and now we have to deal with the terrible consequences of what you've done.'

I thought about that as the rain continued to fall around me.

I wasn't a procrastinator by nature, but in this case, I thought I'd make an exception.

I stuck to the shadows on the jog back to my car.

Chapter Twenty-five

I left the car on Grand Concourse and walked in a daze down 193rd, trying to think my way through this disaster. I met Mike on the south side of the park at the entrance far from where the bosses were set up in the Command Center on Jerome.

I couldn't help noticing the half-dozen news vans parked alongside it. Great. The public has a right to know. To which I have to ask, Why is that?

'Anybody notice I was gone?' I asked Mike in greeting.

He made a pained face. 'Bad news, Lauren. The commissioner came over about ten minutes ago, all outraged about where you were.'

My stomach dropped.

'But you know me,' Mike said. 'I just slapped him around and told him to get his sorry ass back in the donut bus, where he belongs.'

I punched my ever-the-wiseass partner in the arm. The contact felt good, actually.

'I appreciate it,' I said. Mike had no idea how much.

The steady rain continued to fall as we made our way toward the tenements on Creston Avenue on the east side of the park. If two concrete acres of handball courts, rusted basketball hoops, and pit-bull-chewed baby swings could be considered a park.

I don't know what James was the patron saint of, but I have a funny feeling it wasn't the marijuana, coke, and heroin that were sold out of the ancient buildings along the park's perimeter. Judging by the looks of the young, bored-looking hooded men under the red plastic awning of a corner bodega, our presence had slowed sales considerably, though.

'Give me some good news on your canvass, Sarge,' Mike said to a stocky black cop filling out a report in the open door of his double-parked police van.

He looked up, his face disappointed.

Good, I thought. Disappointment was good.

'We got an Amelia Phelps, eighty-year-old African-American lady lives in that rattletrap over there,' the sergeant said, pointing to a vinyl-sided Victorian on the corner.

'She said she saw a car park near her driveway,' the sergeant continued, 'and a man carrying something out of the trunk.'

'White, black, Hispanic?' Mike asked. A loud shout interrupted him.

'THAT'S WHAT YOU GET!'

It was one of the hoodies in front of the bodega. His arms and hands were outstretched.

'FIVE-0 FINALLY GOT WHAT'S COMIN' TO 'EM!' he yelled again. ''BOUT TIME!'

Mike moved out into the street at the bodega so quickly I had to jog to keep up.

'What was that?' he said, putting a hand to his ear as he ducked under the crime-scene tape and closed in on the men in front of the store.

Most of the St James sales personnel had wisely dispersed down the block, but the rabble-rouser, a thin, green-eyed, light-skinned Hispanic, inexplicably stood his ground. He looked to be in his early twenties.

'What? You don't like hearin' the truth?' he said as he cocked his little bantam rooster head at Mike. 'Then do somethin' about it, chump.'

Mike picked up the metal garbage can off the corner and threw it at the guy, two-handed like a basketball pass. Its steel-rimmed side knocked the punk instantly on his back and into the gutter. Mike lifted the can and turned it upside down, burying the kid in garbage.

'How's that for somethin'?' he said.

'He's nothing,' I whispered into my partner's ear after I caught up. 'You want to get jammed up over this mope? Open your eyes, Mike. There's bosses everywhere.'

Mike rubbed the vein throbbing at his temple as he finally let me walk him away.

'You're right. You're right, partner,' he mumbled with his head down. 'Sorry, I lost it.'

That's when I remembered.

Mike was a second-generation cop whose father had been killed in the line of duty. His dad had been a transit cop, and he'd walked into a subway car where a rape was in progress and was shot in the face. It was one of the few cop murders in the history of the NYPD that had never been solved.

So there actually was one thing that could rile my even-tempered partner, I thought as I pulled him toward the witness's house.

A dead cop.

Things just kept getting better and better.

Chapter Twenty-six

H ere was our witness. And what exactly had she seen? Amelia Phelps, tiny, elderly, and black, was a retired Bronx High School of Science English teacher.

'Would you like some tea?' she inquired with perfect diction as she brought us into her dusty, threadbare parlor. Books covered every surface and were piled chest-high like trash in a landfill.

'That's okay, Mrs Phelps,' Mike said, taking out his bifocals and putting them on.

'Ms Phelps,' she corrected him.

'Sorry,' Mike said. 'Ms Phelps, as you know, a police officer was found dead in the park. We're the detectives conducting the investigation. Can you help us?'

'The car I saw was a Toyota,' Ms Phelps said. 'A Camry, I believe, and a recent model. The man who exited it was white, five eleven maybe. He wore glasses and dark clothing.

'At first I thought he was here for the same unfortunate reason most Caucasians visit our community; namely, the purchase of illegal drugs from our neighborhood boys. But then, oddly, I saw him open the back door of his car and emerge with a large something rolled up in a blue sheet. It could very well have been a body. He returned approximately five minutes later, empty-handed, and drove away.'

When I glanced at Mike, he looked as happily astonished as I felt dismayed.

Because this Bronx witness, this former schoolteacher, was a rare species indeed. We'd done midday gas station shootings where not one of twenty people had seen anything. Drive-bys of weddings where both sides of the family hadn't seen or heard a thing. Now, here we had a middle-of-the-night dump job in a drug spot, ostensibly the most difficult of all homicides to solve, and we'd run into photographic-memory Grandma.

'Did you get the plate number?' Mike said expectantly.

No, I thought, wincing. Please God, make her say no.

'No,' Ms Phelps said.

I had to force myself to release my breath silently.

'It was too dark?' Mike said, disappointed.

'No,' Ms Phelps said, looking at him like he was a student who'd forgotten to raise his hand. 'There were no plates.'

'Did you call the police and tell them what you saw?' I said.

Ms Phelps patted me on the knee.

'In this neighborhood, Detective, staying out of other people's affairs is an acquired necessity.'

'Then why did you tell the police officer who knocked on your door that you saw something?' Mike said, curious.

'They asked,' Ms Phelps said with a prim nod. 'I am not a liar.'

That makes one of us, I thought.

'Would you be able to pick out the man you saw from a lineup?' I asked with a tight smile.

'Undoubtedly,' Ms Phelps said.

'Terrific,' I said as I handed Ms Phelps my card. 'We'll be in touch.'

'You can count on it,' added Mike.

Chapter Twenty-seven

Mike had his bifocals on top of his head as we left Amelia Phelps's house and walked back into the park. He mumbled to himself excitedly as he went over his interview notes. He was pumped. He had to feel we were getting closer to the killer. It was a great feeling, I knew. Being a detective, being the good guy.

I missed it terribly.

I felt horrible about lying to Mike and the rest of the cops who were traipsing around in the rain out there. When one cop goes down, all cops feel it. There's the instant outrage, of course, but underneath is unsettling fear. Have I made a mistake in choosing this dangerous job? Is it worth dying for?

I knew my friends and co-workers were reeling, hurting. By telling the truth, I could erase their anxious tension. The thought that somebody else could possibly get hurt out there made me almost physically sick.

I closed my eyes, listening to the crackle of police radio chatter and the rain in the trees.

I didn't say anything to anyone about what I knew, what had actually happened to Scott.

I kept my head down and my mouth shut.

I looked up only when I saw some commotion alongside the fountain.

A couple of dozen uniforms were arraying themselves in parallel lines from the fountain to the medical examiner's black station wagon, waiting underneath the rusted elevated track on Jerome.

'They're taking him out,' I heard one of the uniforms say as he rushed past me to grab a place in the line.

An honor guard of six cops carefully stepped into the water of the fountain and received from the medical examiner's team the green-black body bag Scott had already been placed in. They handled him as if he were a sick person who was still alive. Oh, God, I wished that were true. I wished I could take this entire night back, every second of it.

Along that stock-still, midnight-blue rank, someone started singing 'Danny Boy' in a high, clear, haunting tenor that would have made Ronan Tynan jealous.

You want a definition of *forlorn*? How about half a dozen cops slowly bearing one of their dead through a dark Bronx tenement valley while the rain falls and the pipes, the pipes are calling. Was Scott even Irish? I didn't know. All dead cops are Irish, I guess.

I watched the rain splatter like flung holy water against the body bag as the procession passed me. Everywhere men were weeping openly. I watched as even the commissioner, standing beside the ME office's hearse, cupped a hand over his eyes.

An overhead passing number 4 train sounded out a martial drum snare as Scott was slid into the back of the wagon like a file returned to a drawer.

Tears drained out of my eyes as if my tear ducts had been slit.

Chapter Twenty-eight

I caught a white blur out of the corner of my eye, and suddenly I was enveloped in a wall of warm Tyvek.

'Oh, Lauren,' an academy classmate of mine, Bonnie Clesnik, whispered in my ear as she hugged me to her side. 'This is so horrible. That poor guy.'

Bonnie had been pre-med at NYU before she dropped out to become a cop, and she was now a sergeant in the Crime Scene Unit. As the only female former professionals in a class filled mostly with twenty-two-year-old, smooth-faced boys from Long Island, we had formed a quick bond. I'd stayed over at 'the Bonster' and her partner Tatum's loft on St Mark's Place so many times, they named the futon after me.

Bonnie fished a Kleenex out of her suit and wiped the corners of her eyes, then handed me a tissue, too.

'Look at us,' she said with a laugh. 'Badass cops, huh? It's been – what? A year? You did something to your hair. I like it.'

'Thanks,' Mike said, stepping between us. 'I just washed it. And you are?'

'Bonnie, this fool is my partner, Mike,' I said introducing them. 'I thought you worked days.'

'When I heard the news, I came running, just like everybody

else,' Bonnie said. 'I haven't seen this many cops in one place since St Paddy's. Or Ground Zero.'

She took off the freezer bag that was strapped across her chest beside several cameras.

'I'm glad I did, though, Lauren. I'm really glad. I think I found something.'

I accepted the freezer bag from her, held it up.

Every light in the park and beyond seemed to surge suddenly with a white-hot brightness. The rain felt like it was falling right through me.

I turned Paul's wire-rimmed silver glasses slowly in my hand.

'They were in the sheet Scott was wrapped in,' Bonnie said. 'I already called one of the guys in his narcotics unit. Scott didn't wear glasses. If they're prescription, we can go through the files of every ophthalmologist in the tristate area and nail the four-eyed son of a bitch who did this.'

I felt a tingling behind my left eye as Mike whooped and gave Bonnie a high five.

A stream of electrified chatter leaked from Mike's radio a moment later.

'It's the boss man, Lauren,' he said. 'The commissioner has entered the donut bus and wants a briefing.'

'Are you okay, Lauren?' Bonnie said, putting a hand on my back. 'You don't look so hot.'

I looked at her, at the concern in her eyes. Christ, how I longed to break down right there and then. Bonnie was a friend, a woman, and a cop. Out of everybody, she'd be the most likely to understand. Tell me what to do. Help me.

But what could I say to her? I was screwing the deceased, who, by the way, was blown away by my husband? I looked away from Bonnie. Nobody could help me, I realized. I was completely and utterly on my own.

'I'm fine,' I said.

'We're all a little overwrought,' Mike explained to Bonnie as he led me away toward the Command Center bus. 'Even some of those dealers by the bodega teared up when that red-haired uniform was singing "Danny Boy."'

Mike put his arm around me as we walked. He really was a good guy, one of the best.

'Our man is messing up, Lauren,' Mike said. 'At first I thought we were screwed. You know as well as I do how hard dump jobs are to solve. But look. Mistake after mistake. We're looking at an amateur. I can almost see him out there thinking he's covering his tracks, but his mind is racing and he's fucking up, just leading us closer and closer. A twelve-pack of Sam Adams says we lay hands on his sorry ass by this time tomorrow. You down?'

I shook my head as I labored to stay on my feet, to keep moving toward the bus.

'That's okay, Mike,' I said. 'I don't take sucker bets.'

Chapter Twenty-nine

A short blur of time later, I was making myself stand up straight in the antiseptic glare of the Command Center bus interior.

Everywhere there were cops in front of laptops. White-shirted bosses were barking into cell phones. A map of the area was projected up in a wide-screen PowerPoint display. It looked like the situation room at the Pentagon, or maybe on the TV show *24*.

I could feel my heartbeat pulsing crazily in my eardrums, behind my eyes.

And Paul was the enemy.

'Commissioner,' my boss was saying with a formality I was unaware he was capable of, 'this is Detective Stillwell, the primary investigator on the case.'

A large hand shook mine, and I looked up into the famous, fatherly black face of the police commissioner of New York, Ronald Durham.

'Pleasure to meet you, Detective Stillwell,' Durham said in a warm, honey-laced tone. 'Some of your reports have crossed my desk. You do very good work.'

My God, I thought, feeling dizzy again. My first 'attaboy' from the police commissioner. Put another shelf in the career trophy case.

Then I came down like a crackhead after a three-day binge when I remembered the utterly damning evidence of Paul's glasses.

The cottage cheese in my fridge was going to outlast my career.

'Thank you, sir,' I fumbled.

'Tell me what you have so far,' Durham said next. His eyes were huge and pinned on mine.

I went through it all. Scott's wounds, Amelia Phelps's perfect description of Paul and his car, the glasses we'd just found. The entire homemade recipe for my own disaster.

When I was finished with the speech, the commissioner tapped a forefinger to his lip. Unlike a lot of the top brass, Durham had actually been a detective on his way up.

'Have you looked over his open files?' the commissioner asked.

'I haven't had a chance yet, sir. That's next on our list.'

Durham nodded.

'You're closing in quickly,' he said. 'The only thing that might soften the blow here for everyone is expedience.'

Not everyone, I thought.

'Detective,' the commissioner said, smiling. I knew he was going to ask me for something. What it was, I had no clue. I just knew that in the NYPD, after a boss feeds you a carrot, the stick isn't far behind.

'Sir?' I said, trying to keep the nervousness out of my voice, and failing miserably.

'I wanted to remind you to serve the death notification to Scott Thayer's family.'

My jaw muscle locked and I was surprised my teeth didn't shatter. Jesus Christ, I'd forgotten! Telling the family was part of my job as the primary.

Scott had told me he had a mom and a younger sister somewhere out in Brooklyn. How excruciating was this going to be? Couldn't I just feed my hand into a wood chipper instead?

'Of course, sir,' I said.

'I know it's the most unfortunate part of your job,' Commissioner Durham said with a fatherly pat on my shoulder. 'I just think it should be done before someone leaks Scott's name to the press. I think it would also be better to hear it from some-body out of the same office. Then I could arrive a little later. Help soothe the blow.'

'I understand,' I said.

Then the commissioner sighed.

'Though I know whatever way we do it, it's going to be nothing short of devastating for Scott's wife,' Durham said gravely. 'Not to mention his three young kids.'

Chapter Thirty

Scott was married?

    I managed to stay upright on my suddenly numb legs by a sheer act of will.

A married father of three?

He sure hadn't mentioned that.

Not the wife. Or the kids. Scott had told me he was NYPD's most eligible bachelor.

'I know,' the commissioner said. 'It just keeps getting worse and worse. We have ourselves a real tragedy here tonight. Scott's wife, Brooke, is only twenty-six, and his kids are four, two, and an infant.'

Another fatherly pat on my shoulder signaled that our meeting had come to an end. I had the feeling there must be a section on fatherly pats on NYPD promotion tests.

'Your lieutenant has the address,' the commissioner said. 'Proceed, Detective. Good luck.'

Twenty minutes or so after we left the commissioner in the Command Center bus, we stopped in front of a cute Dutch colonial in the middle of a long block lined with them.

All the windows of the Thayer house were dark. Bright flowers lined a curving slate path through the manicured lawn.

There was a Fisher-Price basketball backboard at the end of the short driveway. I had to tear my eyes away from it. I checked my watch. It was coming up on 4 a.m.

Wait a second, I thought insanely. Did I really have to go into that house? I could just walk away, couldn't I? Forget everything. That I was a cop. That I was a wife. I mean, why be so conventional? I was in the market for a life change. Maybe I could run off to an abbey and make cheese.

'Ready, Lauren?' Mike asked at my side.

'No,' I said, opening the storm door anyway. Then I hit the brass knocker on the inside door a couple of times.

Beautiful, was my first thought when I looked into the groggy face of the petite brunette who answered the door.

Why would Scott cheat on this perfectly lovely young woman? The mother of his kids.

'Yes?' Brooke Thayer said, her eyes widening as she looked from me to Mike and back to me.

'Hi, Brooke,' I said, showing her my badge. 'My name's Lauren. I'm a detective from Scott's precinct.'

'Oh my God,' Brooke said, instantly awake and talking very fast. 'It's Scotty, isn't it? No! What happened? Is he hurt? He's hurt?'

Death notices are served in different ways, none of them pleasant. Some detectives think blunt honesty is the way to go. Others soften the blow by first saying the victim was seriously injured and lead into the fact of their death.

For the first time this night, I went with honesty.

'He was shot, Brooke. I'm so sorry. He's gone.'

I watched her eyes go. That's something you never get used to. Watching someone standing right in front of you disappear. Recede into themselves.

Then she stumbled back away from the door, her legs dancing

side to side like a center fielder trying to get under a fly ball. Finally she dropped to her knees.

'No!' Brooke Thayer screamed.

I found myself on my knees with her in the dark foyer, my hand – my evil, betraying, foul hand – rubbing her thin back as she screamed louder and louder.

'NOOO! NOOO! NOOO!'

'I know,' I whispered in her ear. 'I know.'

'YOU DON'T KNOW SHIT!' she screamed in my face, clawing me away from her. I reared back, covering myself. One of her long nails had raked a red line diagonally across my forehead. Then she collapsed sideways to the floor.

'You don't knoooow!' she cried into the hardwood floor. 'You don't know! You don't!'

Chapter Thirty-one

Mike lifted Brooke Thayer up and put her on the couch in the family room. After I closed the front door, I spotted a blonde girl in pink Disney Three Princesses pajamas. She was staring down at me from the top of the stairs.

'Hey, sweetheart,' I said. 'Your mommy is going to be all right. My name's Lauren.'

The adorable little girl said nothing. She just continued to stare at me with her big blue eyes.

'Maybe you should go back to sleep, honey,' I said, taking a step up the stairs toward her.

She screamed then. In a pitch so high and violent, I had to avert my face and cup my ears.

Brooke shot past me up the stairs, the siren quitting immediately as the girl was scooped up into her mother's arms.

I stood there as the mother and daughter rocked back and forth. On a side table in the living room, I spotted a picture of Scott in his uniform. He had his arm around a pregnant Brooke. It looked like it was taken in a park somewhere. The sun was shining brilliantly.

When Brooke and her daughter started keening at the same pitch, I suddenly thought about the gun in my bag. I visualized it. The way its steel shone like chrome under the light. Its almost feminine curves. I imagined the cold of its barrel placed against my temple, the feel of its hair trigger on the second joint inside my right index finger.

I stood in Scott's house and thought of my gun, and of what I had done, and I wondered how much more of this I could take.

You're not a bad person, I tried to tell myself. *At least you weren't before tonight.*

Chapter Thirty-two

Poor Brooke was still rocking her four-year-old daughter when a baby started crying from somewhere behind them in the upstairs hall.

Slowly, I climbed to the top.

'Do you want me to check on the baby?' I asked Brooke.

Brooke's eyes seemed to stare right through me. She said nothing, not a word.

'Try to find an address book in one of the kitchen drawers and call a family member to come,' I called down to Mike.

I walked past Brooke, following the cries to the nursery at the back of the house.

A mobile of mitts and bats dangled above the crib, and there was a Mets night-light.

The baby boy couldn't have been even six months. I lifted up the tiny wailing child.

His whole body trembled with each cry, a sound that seemed too big for his size. I cupped him against my chest, and he stopped crying almost immediately. I sat down in the rocking chair and held him close, thankful to escape the noise below for a short while.

Even under the wretched circumstances, I noticed how

wonderful he smelled. How pure. I swallowed hard when he finally opened his big eyes. His big, warm brown eyes.

He looked exactly like Scott.

I was the one who started crying then. This baby in my arms no longer had a father, I thought.

Way to go, Lauren. Way to go.

'Give him to me,' Brooke barked, suddenly charging into the room with a bottle. The baby boy seemed to smile at me as I handed him over to his mother. Brooke was still crying, but she seemed to be over the initial shock.

'Can I call someone for you?' I offered.

'I already spoke to my mom,' Brooke said. 'She's on her way.'

She looked straight into my face for the first time. Her brown eyes were surprisingly kind.

'Look,' she said. 'I scratched you. I'm so sorry. I . . .'

'Please,' I said quickly. 'Don't you dare be sorry. You're the one who needs help now. You and your children.'

'I want to hear you say it,' Brooke said after a minute.

I stared at her, wide-eyed. Her features looked stark in the night-light, her eyes a void of shadow.

'What?' I said.

'I want to hear you say what happened to my husband. I appreciated your honesty before. The men will only try to protect my feelings. I need to know exactly what happened so I can try to deal with it. These kids need me to be able to deal with it.'

'We don't really know yet, Brooke,' I said. 'We found him shot in a park, St James Park in the Bronx. It's a known drug area.'

Her face contorted, her lips quivering. Her left eye began to twitch.

'Ooooooh! I knew it,' she finally said, nodding vigorously. '"Undercover's a promotion, Brooke. They always watch my back." Not always, huh, you goddamned idiot.'

I racked my brain about what to say next in the silence that followed. The walls seemed to move in on me. I needed to get out of there. Something ripe was starting to churn in my stomach. I had to have some air.

What would I normally say in an investigation I didn't already know all too much about? I took out my notebook again.

'When was the last time you saw Scott?' I asked her, trying to act like a detective.

'He left around eight tonight. Said he had to go in for a few hours. He kept insane hours. Scotty was almost never home lately.'

'He didn't say specifically where he was going, did he? Was there a phone call that preceded his departure?'

'Not that I can think of this second. No. I don't remember any call.'

All of a sudden Brooke started bawling again.

'Oh God. His poor mom and sister . . . they were so close. They're going to be . . . I don't think I could tell them. No, I . . . Could you? Detective . . . ?'

'Lauren.'

'Could you call her, Lauren? Scotty's mom, I mean. Will you make the call?'

'Of course,' I said.

'Are you from his unit?'

'No,' I said. 'I'm from Bronx Homicide.'

'Did you know Scotty?' she asked then.

In the silence, I listened to the splutter of Scott's son greedily finishing his bottle.

'No,' I said. 'We were out of the same precinct, but we never had the chance to work together.'

'I'm sorry about what happened with Taylor. My four-year-old,' Brooke said. 'She doesn't respond well to strangers. She's autistic.'

I stood there, breathless.

That was it.

It. The thing that finally took me over the top.

'I hope I didn't frighten her,' I heard myself say as I nearly ran out of the room. 'Could I use your bathroom?'

'Down the hall on your right.'

The vomit came up before I made it to the toilet. I threw both taps on to cover the sound of more retching. And left them on to cover the tea-kettle-high primal shrieks that escaped my throat.

I used the entire roll of toilet paper, cleaning up. I actually took out my gun as I sat on the pink-carpeted toilet lid. I wondered if the coroner would put Death by Guilt on my certificate. I finally put the gun away and went downstairs. Not because I didn't want to kill myself anymore. I just thought that Brooke Thayer was having a bad enough night as it was.

In the kitchen, Mike offered to tell the mother.

'That's okay, Mike,' I said, smiling insanely as I dialed the number from the open address book. 'Why break precedent?'

I held the phone away from my ear after I told Scott's mother that her son was dead. I eyed my partner across the kitchen as we listened to the agonized sounds coming from the earpiece.

Mike lifted a crayon-scribbled picture from underneath a *Blue's Clues* magnet on the fridge and shook his head. One of the kids had drawn a two-headed dragon.

'You find the ones responsible,' Brooke said to me as we made our way to the door a few minutes later. The two-year-old boy was up now, too. He was attached to the leg that the four-year-old had neglected. The baby in Brooke's arms started to cry again.

'YOU FIND THEM!' followed us out the door. 'FIND SCOTTY'S KILLER!'

Chapter Thirty-three

Other than Brooke's words still ringing in my ears, our ride back to the Bronx was dead silent.

Scott's multi-agency Drug Enforcement Task Force team was waiting for us in their squad room on the second floor of the 48th Precinct. My Homicide unit was on the fourth. As I made my way up the stairs, I averted my eyes from the doorway of the muster room Scott and I had met in.

The guys in Scott's unit didn't look like typical cops, even to me. For a second, I thought I'd made a wrong turn and stepped in on a skateboarding club meeting.

The DETF boss, DEA agent Jeff Trahan, was tall and had the longish blond hair of an aging surfer. Scott's main backup, or 'leash,' as they called him, Asian-American NYPD detective Roy Khuong, was so baby-faced he probably had trouble buying cigarettes. New York State detective Dennis Marut had the appearance of an East Asian Doogie Howzer. Mountainous, black, draped head to toe in leather and gold, the last team member, Thaddeus Price, looked more like a bodyguard for a gangsta rapper than a DEA agent. I guess that was to his credit.

I stood beneath the buzzing fluorescents, almost wilting under the hard stares of the men.

But after a moment, I realized the expressions were the same ones I'd been seeing all night, looks of loss mixed with anger and shock. Pretty much what I was feeling myself – at least a *part* of what I was feeling.

For a Narcotics team, losing an undercover was a nightmare realized. Like most survivors of homicide victims, they looked like a bomb had just gone off; they were flailing around, looking for some direction, some notion of what to do next.

'We're here to help in any way we can,' Trahan said solemnly after all the introductions had been made. 'Just tell me what we can do for Scott.'

How much longer could I keep this charade up? I wondered as I glanced away from the group's pain to the water-stained ceiling. A passing Long Island-bound eighteen-wheeler rattled a window that appeared to be painted shut in the corner. I took out my notebook.

'What was Scott currently working on?' I said.

Chapter Thirty-four

Trahan took a deep breath and then began. 'Scott was our primary undercover on a case we're making on a couple of Ecstasy dealers from Hunts Point, the Ordonez brothers,' he said. 'The older brother is an Air Force pilot who does supply runs back and forth to Germany. Turns out he's flying back with just a little more than empty skids on his C-One-thirty. Scott made a couple of midlevel buys with them. We were planning a big one, a quarter-of-a-million-dollar deal, for next week, when we were going to bust them.'

'Had Scott been in contact with them recently?' I said.

'He logged a call with them three days ago,' Roy Khuong jumped in. 'But he could have gotten a call tonight – off duty.'

'Would Scott have gone to meet anyone without telling you?' I said.

'Not if he could have helped it,' Roy said. 'But undercover is seat-of-your-pants, dangerous work. You know that, Detective. Sometimes you don't get a chance to call for backup.'

'You're saying Scott could have been approached by someone unexpectedly, asked to accompany them, and he would have had to do it in order to not make them suspicious,' Mike said.

'Exactly,' said Thaddeus Price. 'It happens.'

Trahan added another twist. 'Or Scott could even have been approached by somebody from a previous case. Somebody he'd busted who'd gotten out of jail maybe. That's your worst fear when you're out there on the street. That you're going to be in Burger King with your kid and meet somebody you've already gone over on.'

I heard my partner groan at what Trahan was saying. There were potentially hundreds of suspects in Scott's murder.

'First thing we need to do is bring in these Ordonez brothers for questioning,' Mike said. 'This deal was for big money. They could have picked Scott up early to rob him. Scott was beaten badly. So maybe he was tortured to tell them where the quarter-million was. We need to pick them up. Do we know where these mutts are?'

'The pilot brother, Mark, works out of the Lakehurst Naval Air Station in South Jersey. We'll have the staties talk to his CO and check his apartment in Toms River,' Trahan said. 'But Victor, the younger one, has three or four stash apartments in Brooklyn and the Bronx. Girlfriends and relatives. It'll take a couple of hours to pinpoint where they're at. We'll get up on our wires and see what we can find out.'

'In the meantime,' Thaddeus said, 'I'll get together the files from Scott's previous busts so we can start cross-referencing them with likelies who might have just gotten out of prison.'

'That's a lot of files,' Trahan said, shaking his head grimly. 'Scott had hundreds of collars. He was one of the best undercovers I ever worked with.'

He sure fooled me, I thought, remembering his wife and family.

I turned away from the pain in Trahan's bloodshot eyes. He looked as if he'd lost a best friend more than a co-worker.

'Wait a second,' Detective Marut said. 'Has Scott's family been told? My God, how will Brooke handle it? All those kids. I think four.'

'Three children. We just got back from the notification,' I said. 'And she's handling it about as well as you would expect.'

It sounded like a gunshot went off when Scott's partner, Roy Khuong, suddenly kicked the side of his desk. Paper went flying as he swept the entire contents of the desktop on to the floor before storming out of the room.

Mike shook his head, took out his cell phone, and started dialing a number.

'Who are you calling?' I said.

'Wake up the ADA on call,' he said. 'I'm going to get him to start on the subpoena to bring up the LUDs on Scott's house and cell phones.'

My breath caught. LUDs were local usage details, a printout of the phone company records that would show every phone call to and from Scott's phones.

Including all the times he had called me!

Five minutes later, Mike stopped in the stairwell on our way upstairs to our squad room.

'Lauren, your eyes are gray,' he said.

'What are you talking about? They're blue,' I said.

'I meant the whites of them,' Mike said. 'You've been banging a mile a minute since this thing started. We're in a holding pattern now. It'll be morning before we get a real handle on anything. You live ten minutes away. Why don't you scoot home for a couple of hours of shut-eye. I was scheduled to work this shift. I'll mind the store.'

Part of me didn't want to leave my partner's side, or to possibly miss something on the case. Who the hell knew what would happen next? But out the grimy stairwell window behind Mike, I couldn't help noticing how the streetlights were starting to swim. I was exhausted.

Whoever said moving and divorce were the two most stressful

events in your life never had their husband shoot their lover.

Collapsing wouldn't help things, I decided.

'Okay, Mike,' I said. 'But call me the second you hear anything. Anything at all.'

'Go home, Lauren.'

'Okay. I'm gone. I'm out of here.'

Chapter Thirty-five

I cut my Mini's engine in my garage and was getting out when I heard something weird in the far-right corner. I guess I was a little jumpy, because immediately my Glock was drawn, sights center-massed on the seated figure there.

Until I realized it was Paul.

I clicked on the lights before I finally holstered my weapon.

Paul was snoring in a lawn chair beside his toolbench. On the concrete floor beside him was a bottle of Johnnie Walker Scotch. With maybe one shot left in it.

Oh yeah, and he wasn't wearing any clothes. He was bareass naked.

He was also wasted. Blotto. Three sheets to the wind, as they say. Maybe four.

How bad I was feeling tonight wasn't a fraction of what was going on with Paul, I realized, staring at his troubled, unconscious face.

I knocked off the last shot in his bottle before I tried to shake him awake. No response.

One of his eyes flipped open when I tugged his earlobe. I pulled at his right hand until he stood.

He mumbled something, but I couldn't make it out as I brought him into the house. I'd never seen him so drunk.

I almost threw my back out, trying to steer him into our bedroom. I finally laid him on top of the bed and brought over the wastebasket in case he was sick.

I was just able to make it into the bathroom myself before all the pent-up stress exploded out of me in violent sobs.

Where the hell was all this going? What did I think I was doing, playing dumb in the investigation? This wasn't a game. *Scott Thayer was dead.* Few things on this earth bring down more scrutiny than an NYPD cop getting murdered. Did I think I could bluff my way through this? Was I crazy?

I thought about Brooke Thayer again. Her autistic daughter. The two other kids. I felt poisoned. Evil. I wanted to turn myself in. At this point, I would do just about anything to take this black burden off myself.

But I wasn't the one who would get punished for it.

It was Paul.

So what was I supposed to do now?

Chapter Thirty-six

I still hadn't figured that out when I totally collapsed three minutes later in the shower.

One moment I was standing there, shampooing my hair, and the next I was sitting down hard on the cold porcelain, water pinging off my torso and legs.

I pressed my forehead to the wet tile as the sum of the night's events dripped through me. What made me the sickest was hard to decide. My flat-out betrayal of Paul? Or staring into Scott's dead face? Or maybe staring into his wife's face?

Closing my eyes, I longed crazily for the water to melt me, to let me stream down the floor of the tub and disappear with a gurgle into the drain.

After a minute of that not happening, I lifted my head off the tile and opened my eyes.

This wasn't just going to go away, was it? I needed to do something. But what?

I considered my choices.

First, what would happen if I turned Paul in?

I was an expert on the Bronx criminal justice system. Like any retailer faced with massive volume most of the time, the Bronx DA's office was willing to make a deal with offenders, offer justice at a reduced rate. But the high-profile nature of Scott's case, I realized, would be considered a career-maker for the prosecution. It would be Paul against the system, and the system would make sure that this was one case they would win, and win with a vengeance.

I thought of the mountains of legal bills. The cost of bail for Paul. *If* he could get bail.

Even with the obvious plea of self-defense, the best-case scenario we were looking at was manslaughter, five years of state prison. I shook my head. *Five years.* Whenever I dropped off a prisoner at Rikers, after five *minutes* I longed to do a hundred laps in a pool of antibacterial soap. I winced as I remembered the cattle line in the search room. The sound of crying babies and the beneath-the-table sex in Visitors.

I imagined Paul looking at me over a scuzzy table, disgust in his blackened eyes.

'What's the matter, Lauren?' he would say. 'I thought you liked quickies.'

And if that wasn't horror enough to consider, there was the New York press. What could be more salivating to the tabloids than a love triangle gone wrong, where two cops were involved, one of them now dead! We were looking at long-lasting infamy here.

Loser Hall of Fame material.

Mass-media humiliation.

And let's not forget what would happen to Scott's family. Right now, Brooke was being regarded as a hero's wife. But once the truth got out, that Scott was killed by the husband of the woman he was cheating with, it would be bye-bye crying on the commissioner's shoulder, bye-bye Brooke, bye-bye kids.

My eyes almost bugged out of my head as I considered these particular details.

It would also be so long line-of-duty death benefits for the Thayer family!

I pictured Brooke rocking with her poor daughter. Instead of getting Scott's pension, she would be left with jack squat.

I stood up in the shower. Tried to catch my breath.

My little decision-making meeting was adjourned.

If this were just about me, I would turn myself in. I would go into my room right now, get dressed, and march into my boss's office. I would confess.

But it wasn't just about me. It was about Paul. It was about Brooke.

And most of all her three fatherless kids.

Who was I kidding? There wasn't any choice, at least not right now.

I had to make everything right again.

The water roared in my ears like thunder as I thrust my face under the spray.

But how could I make everything right?

Chapter Thirty-seven

Paul was still snoring when I left for work. I would like to have spoken with him. To say we had a lot to deal with was quite the understatement. But since I didn't think they offered marriage counseling in prison, I decided that instead of waking him up, priority numero uno was getting back to work to see if I had a shot at keeping my husband out of jail.

Mike was writing Scott's name on the bullpen Homicide chart when I stepped into the squad room.

I was more or less happily surprised when I realized nobody was looking at me suspiciously. I guess adrenaline-flooded and terror-struck have a passing resemblance to bright-eyed and bushy-tailed. Through the smeared glass wall of the rear office, I could see my boss, Lieutenant Keane, talking on his desk phone while dialing his cell.

'What do we got?' I said, handing Mike a bodega coffee from the brown bag I was carrying. Starbucks had yet to make inroads into Soundview.

'Shit,' Mike said, flicking the plastic coffee lid sliver across his desk as he sat. 'No sign of either Ordonez. Turns out the pilot's off work until next Wednesday, and he wasn't at his apartment. Of the younger and even scummier brother, Victor, we have no sign at all.'

Mike handed me a file folder.

'Check out the family album.'

The Ordonez brothers were the only children of Dominican immigrants. On the slightly older brother, Mark, the Air Force pilot, there was surprisingly little. A single assault bust when he was twenty-one. But the younger one, Victor, had a crime-ography that was a long and interesting read.

From the age of sixteen, Victor had been in and out of jail, putting up MVP crime stats. Burglary, narcotics sales, attempted rape, assaults of prisoners while incarcerated, possession of a deadly weapon.

But for me, one charge stood out as if it had been marked with a neon highlighter.

Attempted murder of a police officer.

The abstract described how at the age of seventeen, Victor, while resisting arrest for yet another possession charge, drew a concealed .380 semiautomatic, pointed it at the officer's face, and pulled the trigger several times. After he was wrestled to the ground, it was discovered that the gun hadn't discharged due solely to the fortuitous fact that young Victor, new to the wonderful world of semiautomatics, had forgotten to rack the slide and jack the first round into the chamber. To show you what kind of straits the New York criminal justice system was in during the crack epidemic of the early nineties, Victor did just one year.

I blinked down at the sheet in disbelief.

Victor Ordonez was looking so good for Scott's murder, I was almost convinced he'd done it.

I pointed my chin at the file stacks covering both of our adjoining desks and the floor as I sat down.

'Scott's previous Narcotics cases?' I said.

Mike nodded grimly. He chucked his reading glasses on to his desk and rubbed his eyes.

'I'm not cracking spine one of that saga until we have a talk with our Dominican friends,' he said. 'I guess the only good news is I got an ADA to get a subpoena to the telephone company. They're getting Scott's records together right now. They're going to fax it over within the next ten minutes.'

Chapter Thirty-eight

I sat there, rock still, trying to absorb what I had just heard. The fluorescent lights above hummed in my ears like an angry beehive.

How many times had Scott called me in the last month? Twenty? Thirty maybe? How was I going to bluff my way out of this one? I pictured the confusion on my partner's face as he spotted my number over and over again.

Mike moved his mouse to remove his 'Who pissed in your gene pool?' screen saver. It sounded like someone stepping on Bubble Wrap when he rolled his neck.

'Mike, what are you doing?' I finally said.

'Gonna get a jump on those D-D-fives. Keane's about to have triplets. Look at him in there.'

DD5s were the incident reports we had to write for Scott's case file. I raised my eyebrows.

'Um, hello? Earth to Mike,' I said. 'People are going to actually read these reports, Shakespeare. You're the beauty, remember? I'm the brains. In fact, why don't you go grab a couple in the crash room upstairs. We need your head clear just in case we have to knock down a door with it. I'll bang out the reports in a way that doesn't get us reassigned, and when the phone records come in, I'll start collating them. How's that sound?'

Mike stared at me, exaggerated hurt in his red-rimmed eyes. Then he yawned.

'Yes, dear,' he said, standing.

I held my breath as he walked to the exit. The bullpen gate had just swung back into place, when a low, off-pitch ringing sounded.

I turned around. It was the fax machine. *Jeez, Louise.*

It rang again, and the sound was followed by an electronic bleep. One of the white sheets started to slowly slide down into it.

Keep going, partner, I thought, not looking at him. Please. For me.

But out of the corner of my eye, I could see Mike turn around.

My face felt hot. He would see it in a second. My number repeated over and over again! What the hell could I say? Nothing came to mind. How could I get out of this one?

I turned all the way around as Mike lifted the first sheet out. I watched him squint, watched his hand go to his forehead.

That's when I noticed his reading glasses sitting there on the desk beside me, right where he'd left them.

I didn't think. I just acted.

I opened my bottom-left desk drawer, and with one of Scott's files swept Mike's glasses off his desk and into the drawer. Then I quietly kicked the drawer shut.

I pretended to ignore Mike until I heard him rummaging around on his desktop.

'Didn't I tell you to take a nap?' I said, annoyed. 'You're not having another senior moment, are you?'

Mike exhaled a tired breath as he gave up the search for his glasses. He dropped Scott's phone records in my lap.

'All yours, sister,' he said weakly. 'Courtesy of Ma Bell. See you in sixty winks.'

Chapter Thirty-nine

For two solid minutes, I spun my pencil through my fingers like a baton twirler, my old, creaky wooden office chair cawing as I rocked back and forth just staring at Scott's phone records.

I turned and squinted through the office glass at my mercifully still-busy boss, then looked back down at the eight number-filled sheets of paper in front of me.

The fact that I'd managed to get my hands on Scott's records was phenomenal, but after riffling through them, I realized I now had a new problem.

I stuck the pencil between my back teeth and began turning it into a chew toy.

How the hell was I going to remove my number from them?

The thirty-three times it occurred!

'Lauren,' a voice said.

I almost swallowed the pencil's eraser as I looked up. My boss had exited his office and crossed the squad room without my noticing. He placed his hands flat on my desk as he leaned over me, his fingernails practically scratching the edge of the fax paper. Could he read upside down?

'How we looking on those D-D-fives?' Keane said. 'Borough

and Detective Division commanders want them ASAP. Any problem with that?'

'Give me an hour, chief,' I said, bringing the form up on my computer screen.

'You've got half,' he shot back over his shoulder as he left.

I leaned over my keyboard, trying to look busy and at the same time hide what I was doing.

My eyes went from the screen to the phone records. From the phone records to the screen. Waiting for something obvious to jump out at me.

Then, miraculously, it did.

The font of the phone records was a common one. Times New Roman.

A second later, an idea occurred to me all but fully formed.

Which was good, I thought as I clicked on the Microsoft Word icon on my screen, since I didn't have a second to spare.

First thing I did was find the number Scott called the most. It was a 718 area code with an exchange I wasn't familiar with.

I checked my notes and verified that it was Scott's home number.

I typed the number, hit 'print,' and compared it to the records. It was a little too big. I blocked the number out and dropped the font size from twelve to ten, printed that out, and compared it again.

Perfect, I thought. It would work.

I copied the number thirty-three times and hit 'print' for the third time. Who knows? I thought, pocketing scissors and tape from my desk drawer. I lifted the records off my desk along with the sheet from the printer as I stood.

This just might work.

It took me five minutes of nonvirtual cutting and pasting in the last stall of the ladies' room to tape over every incident of my cell number on the LUDs with Scott's home number.

Everything important I learned in kindergarten, I thought as I flushed the scraps away.

One trip to the copying machine later – with a brief side trip to the shredder – and I had everything the way I wanted it.

Scott's new and improved phone records.

I was coming out of Keane's office after dropping off my completed crime-scene reports twenty minutes later when Mike walked back into the squad room. He gaped at the undetectably doctored phone company records I had left on his desk. His reading glasses sat on top of them like a paperweight.

'Don't worry,' I said, giving him a pat on his wide back. 'Dropping a little off your fastball is pretty much expected at your age.'

I lifted my coat from the back of my chair.

'Where are you going?' he said.

'To see my friend Bonnie,' I said. 'Try to speed the crime-scene processing along.'

'Why don't I go with you?' Mike said.

'Because you need to get back to the phone company and put faces to those numbers, see who Scott was calling.'

'C'mon,' Mike said as I was leaving. 'I'll behave. I'm not just a big ugly man doll, you know. I have a sensitive side. I'm in Oprah's Book Club.'

'Sorry,' I said, knocking through the bullpen gate. 'No boys allowed.'

Chapter Forty

C'mon, c'mon, c'mon! Let's go, let's go!
    I checked my watch as a cash register's electronic beep exploded through my skull for perhaps the thirty-seven-billionth time.

I had thought my one-purchase stop at the 57th and Broadway Duane Reade would be quick. But that was before I discovered the aisle-long line behind the lone checkout cashier.

Ten minutes later, I was one customer away from the promised land of the counter when another cashier arrived and called, 'Next.'

Taking the one step needed to the newly opened register, I was nearly mowed down by a middle-aged Asian man in a doorman's suit.

'Hey!' I said.

In response, the line cutter showed me his back, boxing me out as he pushed a bag of Combos at the cashier.

The last thing I wanted was to make a scene, but I didn't have the time to be demure. I leaned in, snatched the Combos out of the cashier's hand, and sent them sailing down one of the crammed aisles behind me. Problem-solving NYC-style.

'Next means next,' I explained to the wide-eyed man as my purchase was scanned and bagged.

I waited until I was in my squad car, double-parked outside on Broadway, to open the bag. I pulled on a pair of rubber crime-scene gloves and took the men's reading glasses out of their package.

The lenses were round, silver-rimmed. Just like the ones Paul had dropped at the crime scene. Just like the ones Bonnie hopefully hadn't processed yet.

I wiped them down with alcohol before snapping open an evidence bag and dropping them in. I lit the receipt with a match and scattered its ashes out the window on to Broadway. Then I turned the engine over and screeched away.

Next stop, police headquarters in Manhattan.

Chapter Forty-one

Bonnie had her head in one of her desk drawers when I stepped into her fifth-floor office at One Police Plaza.

'Hey, Bonnie,' I said. 'That is *you*, isn't it?'

'Lauren, what a happy surprise,' Bonnie said, shaking a bag of Starbucks coffee as she stood. 'And what perfect timing. How about some French roast?'

'So,' she said, placing a steaming black mug in front of me a minute later. 'How are things coming along?'

'I was about to ask you the same thing,' I said.

'Even though this case is our priority, it's going to take some time. All we got so far is that the tarp Scott was wrapped in was a Neat Sheet, a mass-market picnic blanket. They sell them in supermarkets everywhere.'

I sipped my coffee, nodding. I'd bought it at Stop & Shop.

'What about the glasses?' I said.

'Not too much, sorry to say,' Bonnie said. 'There were no visible fingerprints on the lenses themselves. I red-balled them down to the lab to see if they might pick up a partial on the rims, but I wouldn't hold my breath. We're going to have to cross our fingers and see if we can get a hit on a prescription. I just got off the phone with this guy Sakarov, head of ophthalmology at NYU.

He's going to analyze them and guide us through the records.'

I burned my tongue with another sip of coffee, then placed the mug back down on the corner of her desk.

'Do you think I could see them?' I said.

Bonnie gave me a funny look.

'Why?' she said.

I shrugged my shoulders.

'I don't know,' I said. 'To get some sort of feel for this guy. Maybe? You never know.'

Bonnie grinned as she stood.

'Okay, Psychic Detective. The lab's just down the hall. I'll go get them for you. You sit there and prime your mysterious powers until I get back.'

Chapter Forty-two

I fingered the glasses in my jacket pocket as I watched her walk off. My plan was to improvise, but what would I do? Say, 'Look, Bonnie, a bird!' and then do the old switcheroo?

I drank my coffee and tried to think.

About a minute later, a scruffy-looking young man appeared in Bonnie's outer office. I watched him looking around clearly lost. Maybe it was David Blaine, come to give me some sleight-of-hand tips.

I opened the door.

'Can I help you?' I called out.

'I'm looking for Sergeant Clesnik. I'm supposed to pick up a package for Dr Sakarov?'

No! He was here for the glasses. I was out of time.

Or was I? The kid stared at me as I debated. Finally, I took the Duane Reade glasses in the evidence bag from my pocket. I found an empty envelope on Bonnie's desk. I dropped the glasses in, sealed it with a lick, and handed it over.

The kid put the envelope in his shoulder bag and stood there, staring at me. *What now?* Bonnie was going to be back any second.

'Anything else?' I said.

He rubbed the scruff on his chin.

'How about your number?' Shaggy said with a sly smile. 'That'd be cool.'

As if. Like I hadn't had enough of younger men. Now, what could I say that would make him disappear instantly?

'What's your take on kids?' I said, looking into his eyes lovingly. 'Because my four could really use a father figure.'

'Take it easy,' he said with a wave as he finally left.

Bonnie arrived back maybe three minutes later with Paul's glasses in an evidence bag.

'You're lucky you came early,' she said. 'A messenger is about to pick them up.'

'Oh no,' I said. 'Some guy just came in, and I sent him away. Let me run and catch up to him.'

I grabbed the glasses out of Bonnie's hand as I jogged for the exit.

'Thanks for the joe, Bonnie. Call me with the first thing you hear,' I yelled over my shoulder.

Chapter Forty-three

The first important thing I noticed as I stepped back into the Homicide bullpen was that my boss wasn't alone in his office. I had just enough time to put my coat on my chair before his door opened.

'Lauren,' Keane called out. 'Come in here, will you. I need to see you right now.'

I silenced a groan as I walked across the boss's threshold.

Jeff Buslik looked up at me, his dark eyes clear and bright and vigilant.

'Afternoon, Detective,' he said.

For the past five years, the extremely handsome African-American Jeff Buslik had been the Bronx DA's office's homicide bureau chief. Everybody said he was an actual genius. I'd worked with him three times before he'd become head of the bureau, and three times he'd gotten jury convictions. *Bronx jury convictions*, slam-dunked with maximum sentences, state prison, twenty-five years to life.

I rubbed my eyes as I sat down.

'What do you have so far?' the prosecutor said. 'Let me hear it all, Lauren.'

'Give me a break, Jeff,' I said. 'You have my report right there in front of you. Speed-read it again. It'll be quicker.'

Jeff smiled. No wonder juries liked him. He looked like a freaking movie star. He had the gift of glib, too.

'Humor me,' he said.

So I told him.

When I was done, he leaned back on his chair's back legs. He laid his hands on the lapels of his spotless gray suit as he stared up at the water-stained drop ceiling. His half-lidded eyes moved back and forth as if he were reading something. How many homicides had crossed his desk? I wondered. A thousand? Two thousand?

Already he was analyzing and sorting, building up the strengths and weaknesses of the case.

Or maybe he was just reading my mind, I thought, stilling the *tap-tap* routine my shoe had started against the floor. Christ, he made me nervous.

'This elderly witness Amelia Phelps, does she seem believable?' he said after a minute.

I nodded. 'Very believable, Jeff.'

'Pathology report?'

'They're rushing it,' my boss said. 'But it'll still take at least a week.'

'What's your gut on these two dealers?' Jeff said. 'The Ordonez brothers?'

'They're looking damn good,' Keane said. 'Only we're having trouble locating them.'

'You think maybe they could be heading back to the Dominican Republic? *I* think maybe.'

Wouldn't that be lovely? I thought.

'Who knows?' I said.

'Do you think these gentlemen are dumb enough to have the murder weapon on them?' Jeff said, creaking the chair back and forth with a flexing wingtip. 'My juries love murder weapons.

Murder weapons and DNA. Have to give them a crossover episode of *CSI* and *Law and Order* these days. You know that. We find the gun, hopefully with a little blood on it, it'll be over before it starts.'

A vivid picture of the gun and the bloody bag in my toolshed flashed through my brain.

'I've worked in this borough for a while, Jeff,' I said nonchalantly. 'Dumb is something I never underestimate.'

Jeff gave me some more red-carpet wattage as he smiled broadly again.

'You seem to have your end covered as usual, Detective,' he said. 'I'll head back to the office and get started on boiler-plating some search warrants. Soon as you get an address, we'll be ready to go. Maybe shoot for the death sentence on this one.'

Chapter Forty-four

I nearly imploded in my desk chair after Jeff Buslik left the building. I thought I could handle this. Because I was in charge of the case, I thought I could get out in front of everything. Now I wasn't sure. In fact, I doubted it.

I'd been lucky so far, but how much longer could that last? Not long with clear-eyed Jeff Buslik staring over my shoulder. He could sense guilt the way a shark can smell blood.

Twenty minutes later, Mike came in with a dozen Dunkin' Donuts and a Box o' Joe.

Wow, a keg of caffeine. I wasn't high-strung enough yet?

'What's the word?' I said.

Mike shook his head.

'Jelly?' he said, opening the box. 'Nobody knows squat. It's hurry-up-and-wait time. Boston cream?'

The rest of the day and into the night was spent 'no commenting' the reporters, who called by the half-hour, and flipping through Scott's case files.

Scott had really been a terrific undercover, I soon discovered. He'd been loaned out on stings to the FBI and the ATF and had actually gotten to be the right-hand man of a high-level guy in the Cali cartel.

I found a picture of him smiling along with the rest of his inter-agency task force as they posed in front of a white sandbag wall of seized cocaine. *Oh, Scott.*

I shook my head as I slapped the file closed and opened another.

A born bullshit artist, I thought, and I actually had to go ahead and believe him.

The next time I looked up, the squad room windows were dark. What time was it?

Mike hung up his phone and growled like a bear awakened from hibernation two months early.

'Get this. These DEA geniuses have the Brothers Ordonez's location, and I quote, "pinned down to this after-hours club they partially own in Mott Haven or to an apartment in the ass end of Brooklyn."'

'That's some *or*,' I said.

'My sentiments exactly. Bottom line, we're looking at a long night,' Mike said. 'It's your turn to crash. Go home and see what that husband of yours is looking like these days. Keep your cell phone on. The second I get the word, you'll get it. Go home.'

Chapter Forty-five

I heard the TV in the den when I came in. A lone voice followed by studio audience laughter. Letterman, probably. Great. He'd be doing a Top Ten about me and Paul soon enough.

I put my keys on the pub mirror and looked at the blue TV light spilling through the crack on to the runner of carpet in the hall. Of all the difficult things I'd done all day, this one felt like the hardest.

Nothing could quite top off a long day of covering up a murder like having to admit to your husband that you cheated on him.

I took a long lungful of oxygen, slowly let it out, and pushed the door open.

Paul was lying on the couch with a Yankees throw pulled up to his chin. He clicked off the set when he saw me standing there.

'Hey,' he said with a smile. He still had a nice smile, even at the most inappropriate times.

I stared at him. I don't know what I was expecting, but a cheerful 'hey' wasn't it. 'Hey, slut' maybe.

'Hey, yourself?' I said tentatively.

I didn't know what the next dance step was supposed to be. Not even a wild guess. I'd never had Paul murder my lover before.

'How was work?' Paul asked me.

'Work was fine, Paul,' I said. 'Um, don't you think that maybe we should talk a little bit about last night?'

Paul lowered his eyes to the floor. Now maybe we were getting somewhere.

'I was pretty loaded, huh?' he said.

That's what generally happens when you practically polish off a bottle of Scotch by yourself, I wanted to say. But I guess I needed to be supportive. I definitely needed Paul to open up, unburden himself. Tell me exactly what happened. His side of things.

It would make things so much easier. He could get it off his chest, and I could tell him that he didn't have to worry, that I was already taking care of everything.

'What's going on, Paul?' I whispered. 'You can tell me.'

Paul glanced at me, his lower lip caught between his teeth.

'My God, Lauren,' he said. 'My flight. It was a nightmare. There was this loud boom, and we started plummeting. I was convinced it was another terrorist attack. That I was dead. Then it just stopped. The plane leveled out, but the pilot landed it in Groton. I never made it to Boston.

'It was like I'd been spared, you know? After we touched down, I rented a car and drove home. I guess I was still in shock when I got back in. I opened the bottle to have a drink to calm myself, and pretty soon the bottle was my drink. Don't ask me what happened to my clothes. Sorry. I didn't mean to scare you.'

My face burned in the dark. Why was Paul lying to me now? Acting as if he wasn't aware I knew what was going on? On the other hand, it wasn't uncommon for murderers to enter a state of denial. Sometimes it was so impenetrable, it was like they themselves truly believed they didn't commit the crime. Was that it? Was Paul in shock and so racked with guilt that he'd become delusional?

'Paul!' I finally said. 'Please!'

Paul looked up at me, confused.

'Please what?' he said.

My God, I thought. As if this wasn't hard enough. Was Paul playing some type of game with me? It was as if he didn't know I'd been there too. That he thought Scott had been alone and . . .

Holy shit! That was it! A hand went to my gaping mouth. I couldn't believe it.

Paul didn't know that I'd been there!

He hadn't come to confront us, I realized. He must have seen an e-mail or two, suspected what was going on, and gone over to Scott's to deliver an ass-kicking in order to scare him away from me. That was why he'd left without confronting me! And that was why he was acting oblivious now. He wasn't acting. Paul *was* oblivious!

Paul didn't know I'd cheated on him.

Chapter Forty-six

Now that changed things, didn't it? I stared across the room as Paul lifted up the throw.

'Get in here with me, Lauren,' he said. 'You've been working too hard. Hell, we both have. C'mere.'

Seeing him lying there like that reminded me of the time when I'd thrown out my back chasing a suspect down a Throgs Neck fire escape the year before. I was laid up for two weeks, and Paul had used his vacation to take care of me. *Really take care of me.* He'd cooked us three meals a day, and we'd eaten here together watching daytime TV, reading, Paul reading to me. The water heater gave up the ghost in the middle of the second week, and I'll never forget how Paul washed my hair in the kitchen sink with water heated from the stove.

Bottom line was, he'd been there for me.

Now he needed me to be there for him.

I took a breath and stepped over and lay down beside him. Paul switched off the light. I reached out in the dark until I found his hand, then I held it tight.

'Well, I'm glad you made it home to me,' I finally said. 'Even if your clothes didn't.'

Chapter Forty-seven

The next morning, I got dressed quickly after Paul left for work. I'd been waiting for him to leave, actually. More accurate: I couldn't wait for him to go.

As I was about to dump my handbag into my Mini, I suddenly very distinctly remembered what ADA Jeff Buslik had said about the gun used to kill Scott. *How it was absolutely critical to proving the case.*

I moved away from the car and hurried toward the toolshed, a single question racing through my brain.

Which river was I going to dump the gun in – the Hudson, the East, or the Harlem?

But I swallowed hard as soon as I unlocked the shed's door. I hadn't been expecting this. Not in my wildest dreams.

There was an empty space where the bag of evidence had been! There was just air.

I looked behind the rakes, the bags of fertilizer, the watering can. No gun. No bloody paper towels. No nothing.

What now?

I stared at the spot, wondering what Paul might have done with the murder gun. Had he dumped it when he went to return the car? If so, where?

That worried me. A lot. The murder weapon still around some-place, probably with Paul's prints on it.

I was standing there, stomach churning, when I noticed the shovel. The tip of its blade was dark. I touched it. It was wet with mud. I took it out of the shed with me and jogged toward the backyard.

Where would I bury a murder weapon if I were Paul? I thought.

I'd want to hide it someplace close, I decided. Someplace where I could glance out my window and see if the area had been disturbed.

I scanned my backyard. It got only afternoon sun, so it was still shaded. I paced its entire length, staring at the cool, shadowed ground for twenty minutes, but there were no obvious distur-bances. Not in the plant beds, not beneath the hedges or azaleas.

About ten minutes later, next to the grill, beside a stack of garden bricks we'd bought at Home Depot a year before, I noticed something a little curious. To the right of the pile, I could see faint indentations of bricks in the dirt.

The bricks had been moved slightly over to the left, I realized.

I began removing the top row of bricks and placing them back in their original formation. Under the last row, the earth was loose.

I dug with the shovel until it squished into something. My breath caught and my heart pumped with relief. It was a plastic Stop & Shop bag. I opened it and saw the .38 sitting on top of the bloody towels.

I put the gun in my purse and tied the shopping bag and put it in the trunk of my Impala, the cop car I usually drove to work in. Then I went back, filled the hole, and painstakingly put the bricks back the way I'd found them.

I was sweating, placing the last brick back down, when I heard something at the corner of the house.

I turned.

And my heart stopped.

It was my partner, Mike.

Mike? Here at my house? Now?

Behind him were Scott's DETF group members Jeff Trahan and Roy Khuong. All three were wearing full ballistic armor.

I could feel my sweat glands open like a drain. This was it – endgame!

They'd been surveilling me, I thought. They knew exactly what had happened. Probably from the get-go.

Now it was over.

My mouth opened wordlessly as I stared at them from where I was, on my knees.

'What's up, Lauren? Don't you answer your phone?' Mike said, pulling me up. 'We just got word from a confidential informant that the Ordonez boys are at their club right now. We decided to just come by and pick you up. Marut and Price are waiting in the van.'

He slapped the dirt from my hands as if I were a naughty child he'd caught playing in the mud.

'You can plant your perennials later, Martha Stewart,' my fired-up partner said with a grin. 'It's time for us to bag some cop killers.'

Chapter Forty-eight

Riding in the back of a speeding van disguised as a plumbing company's, which the Bronx Narcotics Drug Enforcement Task Force used for surveillance, I studied the black-and-white photographs of the Ordonez brothers that Mike had brought with him. The pilot, Mark, was a year older than his brother, Victor, but the hard-eyed, pock-marked tough guys could have been twins.

I handed the pictures back to Mike, who was crouched next to me. He was sheathed in Kevlar, a tactical shotgun held port arms across his chest. I was wearing a full vest, too, and it felt incredibly heavy across my back and shoulders.

Or maybe it was just my head-about-to-explode guilt and anxiety dragging on me.

'Couple of real lookers,' I managed to get out.

'Did you notice how light-skinned Victor is? Six foot. He matches Amelia Phelps's description almost to a T. He did it, Lauren. He's our guy. He just about killed a cop fifteen years ago, and he finally got his chance with Scott. The son of a bitch was Scott's shooter. I can feel it.'

I stared at my partner. There was a far-off look in his eyes, a malevolent gaze. 'These two are going to wish their mother strangled them at birth,' he whispered.

I raked my hair back with my fingers. I remembered again that Mike's dad had been killed on The Job. Now we were going after cop killers. I wondered suddenly if this was such a good idea. Actually, I knew it wasn't.

'We're here,' Trahan called from the wheel as the van slowed. 'Lock and load, ladies.'

There was a heady metallic smell in the van's enclosed space. Adrenaline probably. Or maybe testosterone. Things were happening way too fast. The click of weapons echoed off the stark steel walls.

We were parked on East 141st Street somewhere off Willis Avenue. I guessed the Manhattan real-estate bubble had yet to blow in this direction, looking out at the weed-filled lots and crumbling buildings.

Anything to keep my mind off what was happening now.

Across the desolate street, a wind-blown page of *El Diario* caught against the skeletal bumper of a stripped-to-the-bones Escalade. The only structures that looked semi-sound around here were the housing projects across the gun-metal strip of the Harlem River behind us.

Trahan pointed at an ancient, listing four-story walk-up midway down the block.

'There she blows,' he said. 'That's the club.'

Club? I thought, confused. What club? What Trahan was pointing at were just two graffiti-covered steel shutters book-ending the shadowed doorway of an anonymous-looking store-front. The crumbling tenement windows above it were empty. Not just of people. Of glass and aluminum frames too.

Trahan caught my dumbfounded look.

'You have to see this place inside,' he said with a rueful shake of his head. 'It's another world.'

Trahan took out his cell phone and made a call. He *tssked* after a few seconds, snapped it shut.

'Damn confidential informants,' he said. 'She's not picking up.'

'It's a woman?' I said.

'Of course,' Detective Marut said. 'She was sleeping with Mark Ordonez until he left her for another lady. There's no better informant than a woman scorned.'

'When did you last hear from her?' I asked.

'Right before we picked you up,' Trahan said. He bit the antenna of his radio in frustration.

'I wanted to hit it fast, flash-bang through the front door, get everybody down. Now I'm not so sure. My CI there said that the place was packed. We can't risk somebody getting hurt, especially us, unless the Ordonez brothers are definitely in there. Then, fuck everything!'

'Hey, wait a second,' I said. 'Where's the Emergency Service Unit? They live for this kind of stuff. Why don't we let them handle it?'

'Scott was our brother,' Khuong said gravely, his eyes hard and dark as coal. 'This stays in the family.'

Good Lord. I didn't like the sound of that. I was getting a scary vibe off everyone, actually. These guys were too keyed up. Letting their emotions get the best of them. This thing felt more like a war party than an arrest procedure. Whatever happened to removing the emotionally involved from the case? Like I of all people should talk.

'Did somebody say that the place was packed?' I said, staring dubiously at the desolate establishment. 'It's coming on nine a.m.'

Thaddeus's gold tooth winked. At least I think that's what I saw. He racked his 10mm Smith & Wesson.

'Some people never want the party to end, girl,' he said.

'Wait a second. How are we going to do a recon?' Detective Marut chimed in. 'If these guys killed Scott, then they're going to be superparanoid about anybody who looks suspicious. We've all been on surveillance. Who knows if they made us?'

'I have an idea,' I said.

I stared at the club. It looked evil, like an inner-city entrance to Hell. But I was the one whose charade had put us here, and I could barely live with myself at that moment. If somebody else got hurt, I didn't know what I would do.

'Wire me up,' I said.

Trahan shook his head. 'No way.'

'What are you, nuts?' Mike said. 'No way are you going into that pit alone. I'll do it.'

I stared into my partner's eyes. He meant what he'd just said. Like I said, he's the best.

'You listen to me,' I said. 'I'm going in. They don't know me from Eve. They won't expect a woman. Oh, and if that's not good enough for you, I'm the primary investigator. And to answer your first question, yes, obviously I'm nuts.'

Chapter Forty-nine

It took about a minute and a half for DEA agent Thaddeus Price to attach a tiny wireless Typhoon mike under the button of my suit jacket. I kind of wanted to tell him I wasn't in that big a hurry, but I kept that particular news flash to myself.

'Okay, here's the set,' he said. 'This place is a shithole, but believe it or not, on Friday mornings they get a slumming, hard-partying Manhattan crowd. Go up, knock on the door, and tell the bouncer you're looking for your boyfriend, DJ Lewis. Don't worry, he's not there. But the bouncer will probably let you in.'

'Why's that?' I said.

Thaddeus's tooth glittered again as he smiled at me.

'Look in the mirror, Detective. Pretty white girls like you don't need to be on the list.'

'You see either of our buddies, Mark or Victor,' Trahan advised, 'I want you to call out, "Code red," and find the nearest corner. Same goes if there's trouble, if you feel you're in any danger at all. We'll be there before you can draw another breath, okay?'

'Code red,' I said. 'Got it.' Hell, I'd been in code red for the past twenty-four hours.

'All right, what else?' Trahan said. 'Oh yeah. Cough up your weapon and badge. The bouncer might want to search you.'

The walls of the cramped van suddenly seemed to shrink in on me, until I felt like I was lying in a coffin. My own coffin.

Dear Holy Christ!

I could hand over my Glock and badge without any problem whatsoever.

But Scott's gun, the one that Paul had used to murder him, was in my handbag. That might raise a few eyebrows in the van. What the hell was I going to do now?

I reached into my purse and handed Trahan my Glock. Then I gave him my gold badge.

But I left Scott's murder weapon right where it was, under my wallet and a box of Altoids. 'Wish me luck,' I said.

'Code red,' Trahan repeated. 'Don't be a hero in there, Lauren.'

'Trust me, I'm no hero.'

The door of the van suddenly slid open, and I stepped out, blinking, on to the cracked and stained sidewalk. I looked around. I didn't know which was bleaker, the inner-city horizon or my dwindling chances of pulling this crazy charade off alive.

'Don't worry, partner,' Mike said. 'We'll be watching you every step of the way.'

Yeah, I thought, hefting my bag as the door slammed shut.

That was precisely the problem.

I stared at the establishment in question, the so-called club. The steel shutters. The lightless doorway between them like a vertical open grave.

What in the name of everything holy could happen to me next?

Code red was the least of my problems.

Chapter Fifty

In the small alcove just inside the crummy front door was a crimson velvet rope, and behind it, an ink-black stairwell leading down.

The bouncer standing next to it was wearing champagne-colored sunglasses and a three-piece suit that could have been made of red Mylar. I silently debated what made me more uneasy as I approached him, the fact that he was six and a half feet tall or the fact that he was morbidly obese.

A steady thumping rose from the raw concrete stairwell at his side, as if blasting were going on in the depths of the earth.

'Lewis spinning tonight?' I asked.

The bouncer shook his huge head almost imperceptibly.

Did he understand English? Did he automatically know I was a cop? I felt suddenly very glad Mike and the other guys were just a yell away.

'Is it a private party, or can I get in?' I said.

Private party, I prayed, glancing down into the black of the stairwell. I had no problem with going back to the van a failure. We could figure something else out. I was leaning toward a nap at that point. Or maybe a three-week vacation out of the country.

'Depends.' The bouncer finally spoke.

'On what?' I said.

The bouncer lowered his shades and adjusted himself in a way that made me glad I hadn't eaten any breakfast.

'On how bad you want in,' he said.

'That's really romantic,' I said as I turned on my heel. 'But there's nothing on this earth I want that bad.'

'Come back, come back,' the unsavory bouncer said, booming nasty laughter as he unclipped the velvet rope. 'Don't get so testy, white girl. Just a little joke. Bouncer humor. Welcome to Wonderland.'

Chapter Fifty-one

I was almost ready to draw Scott's gun for protection by the time I made it to the bottom of the treacherously dark stairwell. Instead, I took a deep breath. Then I stepped toward the amplified throbbing, passing through a doorway curtained with crystal beads.

On the other side, I stared, amazed, at the flat-screen TVs, the expensive lighting, the packed center bar that looked like it was made of black glass.

The female bartenders behind it wore black rubber cat suits and fake breasts. Heck, they might have been transvestites. The Bronx really was back.

I had to admit, I was kind of impressed. This could have been Manhattan. The Ordonez brothers had done their degradation research.

Among the predominantly Hispanic crowd was a well-represented contingent of upscale white people. They were sweating on the dance floor, faces rapt with foolish smiles as they spun neon-colored glow sticks in both hands.

Above the gyrating dancers, in a steel cage suspended from the ceiling, a naked dwarf wearing angel wings was banging on the bars with a white nightstick. Who thinks this shit up? I wondered.

'I can feel your energy,' a bloated middle-aged bond-trader-type said as he spilled off the dance floor and went to embrace me.

I tried to stiff-arm him away, and when that didn't work, I lightly kneed him between the legs.

'Now you can – maybe,' I said as he backed off in a hurry. I fled toward the bar.

'Twelve dollars,' the bartender said after I ordered a Heineken.

Look at that, I thought, coughing up the money, they even had Manhattan prices.

Maybe thirty seconds later, a short, pudgy Hispanic man with a goatee smiled and wedged himself in beside me.

'I'm the candy man,' he said.

I stared at him. The candy man? Was that a new pickup line? I'd been out of it for a while. Actually, to tell the truth, nice Catholic girl that I was, I'd never actually been in it.

He placed an ivory-colored pill in my hand. I didn't think it was a Sweet Tart.

'Twenty,' he said.

I gave it back to him and watched him shrug his shoulders and leave. The Ecstasy dealer had to be working for the Ordonezes, right? But I lost him when he stepped into the laser-light kaleidoscope of the dance floor.

I looked around for either Ordonez. I scanned the A-list booths at the rear of the dance floor behind the DJ. The strobes and violent waves of bass weren't exactly helping my concentration. Like it or not, I had to get closer.

I was skirting the far edge of the dance floor to avoid any more unwanted advances when one of the doors in the concrete wall beside me opened.

Victor Ordonez stepped out, staring right into my eyes. Before I could move, an iron hand was wrapped around the back of my neck.

I turned and saw my buddy from upstairs, the bouncer in dire need of Jenny Craig. 'It's only me, lady,' he said, and grinned.

'Why don't you come into the VIP room?' Victor yelled over the music as I was pushed inside. 'Private party. But you can be my guest.'

Chapter Fifty-two

The back VIP room was actually a tenement basement. Raw concrete walls and floors, cinder-block window frames, the rusted hull of an old boiler. Nice decor. A naked bulb hung above an old grease-caked kitchen table that held a stainless-steel electronic scale.

Beyond the table, through a dark doorway, was a corridor with something lying on the floor.

I swallowed hard.

It was a crud-stained mattress.

'Get your filthy hands off me right now,' I said, struggling to break the bouncer's grip.

'Calm down, please,' Victor said pleasantly as he stepped in front of me. He was wearing a three-piece white suit, a white shirt, and a black tie. I wondered if Mickey Rourke knew one of his suits was missing.

'This is a routine security matter,' Victor explained. 'My employee, Ignacio, forgot to search you upstairs. An oversight on his part.'

An alarm bell went off in my head. I wondered what else was routine for the violent drug dealer standing in front of me.

'Hey,' I said. 'Go ahead and kick me out for breaking your rules.

I was thinking about hitting a diner for some breakfast anyway.'

Victor sighed. Then he nodded at the bouncer.

My handbag was ripped away. I heard its contents being dumped on to the table as I scanned the room for another exit.

I couldn't stop staring at the mattress. Or remembering the attempted rape arrest on Victor's rap sheet.

Should I just grab for Scott's gun? I wondered. How many rounds were left? Four? Double-tap Victor, go for a head shot on the behemoth, then get out the same door I came in.

'What's this?' Victor said, picking up Scott's .38 before I could.

I almost panicked. I had an open mike, and I couldn't let the team hear about the gun. I thought quickly. 'That looks like a code red,' I said casually.

'What do you mean, "code red"?' he asked.

'That. The gun you pulled and have pointed at me. *That looks like a code red!*' I said in a loud voice, hoping my mike had picked me up.

My knees stung as Victor suddenly threw me to the floor.

'Shut up, you bitch! Who are you to come into my place, shouting your head off at me?' he yelled.

'*Coño!* Don't you see?' the bouncer behind me said. 'That's a cop gun. She's a fucking lady cop. And Pedro already sold to her!'

'Shut up, you useless hump, and let me think!' Victor screamed.

My face went numb as the younger Ordonez suddenly pointed the gun at me. I stared into the black barrel. Instead of seeing my entire life, everything that had happened since I'd decided to be with Scott flashed before my eyes. In high-definition clarity, I saw every misstep that had led me from two nights before to here and now.

Wait a second, I thought. Where are the troops? I looked at the thick walls. These damn basements! I must have been in a radio blind spot.

'*Code red!*' I screamed as I scrambled for the door.

The bouncer was surprisingly quick for a mountain. I made it only halfway before he grabbed my ankle and almost tore off my entire left foot.

Then there was a scream – and the door exploded!

Pounding dance music instantly flooded the room. My eyes – tearing in the dust and splinters – were greeted with hands-down the most satisfying sight of my life to that point.

My partner, Mike, shotgun to his shoulder, was riding the knocked-down door into the room like it was a surfboard.

Chapter Fifty-three

Mike crushed the bouncer's ugly face with a shotgun butt to the nose before the monster could even form his first curse word.

'Where's Victor?' Mike then said, tossing me my Glock and cuffs. 'We lost your transmission outside. Trahan's informant told us Victor brought you in here.'

'I don't know where he went, Mike,' I said, searching behind me. 'He was right here a second ago.'

'Cuff that one to something and give me some backup,' Mike said. He leveled his shotgun toward the dark passageway where the mattress lay and then rushed toward it.

I cuffed the unconscious bouncer to one of the boiler's pipes. His glasses were shattered and his leaking face was now the color of his suit. Just a little cop humor, I felt like telling him as I ran into the corridor after my partner.

I heard the sound of a door slamming ahead of me.

Where the hell had Mike and Ordonez gone? I banged my shin on some unseen stairs and jogged up them, my Glock leading the way.

The door I finally found, pretty much with my face, exited on to a field with high weeds and garbage and broken glass. Now where was I?

I blinked in the sudden blinding daylight. I saw Mike already halfway across the abandoned lot. A half-block in front of him, a figure in a white suit was sprinting along 140th Street. It was either Victor Ordonez or an ice-cream man training for the marathon.

I began closing the distance as Mike chased Victor east for two blocks. At the end of the third intersection, they went under an elevated track and in through the gate of a junkyard. Would Ordonez get away? I guess I hoped so. If it were up to me, he could keep running until he got back to Santo Domingo.

Unfortunately, Mike kept up his pursuit, rushing hell-bent for glory around an obstacle course of crushed boxes and piled metal. All Ordonez had to do was wait and fire, and Mike would be toast. But it didn't happen that way.

Approaching a rusted tin wall at the rear of the junkyard, I heard a loud metal screech. Then a metal-on-metal boom. *What the hell was that?*

Half a block away, in the farthest corner of the yard, I spotted Ordonez scrambling off the forklift he'd just crashed into the fence.

He dropped to his hands and knees and crawled out of sight through a crack that he'd made in the fence.

A second or two later, Mike appeared from a wall of pipes and dove through the same hole in the fence, still chasing Ordonez.

When I finally got there, huffing and puffing, I could see trains. Lots of trains. Ordonez had fled from a junkyard into a subway railyard.

And I forgot to fill my MetroCard, I thought as I crawled through the fence, keeping my eyes peeled for the deadly third rail.

Chapter Fifty-four

I was running through a narrow space between two parked
number 4 trains, searching frantically for Mike and Ordonez,
when I heard a sharp crack. Shit! The window above my head
shattered. 'Hey, white girl! *Catch!*'

I turned in time to watch Victor Ordonez, who was leaning out
the conductor's window two cars away, fire again. I felt something zip past my ear and then heard a sound like thin ice breaking.

I started emptying my Glock in Victor's direction.

I ejected the empty clip before I realized something warm was
running down my neck. My legs dematerialized suddenly, and I
found myself lying on gravel. There was something wrong with
the side of my face.

God, I'd been hit! I felt dizzy. Like I was sliding out of myself,
watching myself from a distance.

Don't go into shock, Lauren. Move! Do something! Right now! I
scrambled upright and began retreating as fast as my shaky legs
would carry me. I pressed the sleeve of my jacket to my head
where it was bleeding.

I fell to my knees one more time and had to pick myself up
again before I reached the end of the train.

I spotted an open door at the end of the last car. I climbed up, pulled myself inside on my stomach, and rolled under some seats.

That's when the shooting really got started! Two or three cars away, I heard a shotgun blast three times in quick succession. Then it went off again almost on top of me, and the window glass of the car I was in shattered.

I was lying there, curled up on the filthy floor, bleeding and shivering, when from the next car I suddenly heard Ordonez scream. I couldn't see him from where I lay, but I could hear him as clearly as if he were in the same room.

'Okay! Okay! I give up!' Victor Ordonez yelled at somebody.

There was the sound of something heavy dropping against the floor. Scott's gun?

'I want my lawyer,' Ordonez said.

For a second, everything was quiet. Too quiet. What was happening now?

Then a shotgun was jacked.

Click-clack.

'Only thing you're going to need, you cop-killing piece of shit,' I heard Mike say, 'is an undertaker.'

No! I remember thinking. Dear God, Mike. What are you doing? No!

I spun on to my stomach, struggled to stand, my mouth gaping to shout at Mike.

'Cop killer?' I heard Ordonez say with confusion in his voice.

Then the shotgun exploded one last time.

Chapter Fifty-five

I must have passed out for a little while, because the next thing I heard was somebody asking, *'Where the fuck are you?'* The words were coming out of Mike's radio, which lay beside my head. Mike was on the subway car floor, cradling me in his lap.

'You're going to be all right, Lauren,' Mike said. He had a smile on his face, and there were tears in his eyes. 'Your head got nicked. Flesh wound. Honest to God. You're going to be fine.'

'I'm not dying?' I asked Mike.

'Nope. Not on my watch.'

Through the open door between cars, I could see a hand sticking out of a sea of shattered glass. Blood was flecked on a white sleeve.

'What about Victor?' I said. 'You . . .'

Mike put a finger to my lips.

'Fired on him after he shot at me. You remember what happened, partner?'

I winced. I couldn't believe it. Somehow I'd gotten from my normal life to here.

'That's the way it happened. He shot and then I shot,' Mike repeated. 'That way and no other way.'

I nodded, looked away from Mike. 'I hear you. I got it, Mike.'

'They're here,' a frantic voice called from somewhere outside the subway car. 'They're in here.'

'My dad was killed on a train just like this one,' Mike said in a tired voice. 'Just like this one.'

Outside came the *chop-chop* of an approaching helicopter, then the sound of barking dogs.

'He used to take me and my brother fishing out on City Island,' Mike went on. 'My little brother was so hyper he flipped the boat on us one time. I thought my dad was going to drown him, but instead he just laughed. That's how he was. How I'll always remember him. With us hugging his big neck as he laughed like hell, swimming us ashore.'

An awful sound ripped from the back of Mike's throat. Thirty, forty years' worth of grief.

'I always knew something like this would happen,' he said. 'Sooner or later.'

I patted my partner on the elbow.

Then EMTs and cops and DEA agents all came flooding into the shot-up train car.

Chapter Fifty-six

I definitely wasn't dying today. It turned out I didn't need stitches, so the EMTs cleaned my wound, applied pressure to stop the bleeding from my cheek and left ear, and fixed me up with a small bandage. I sat on the edge of the ambulance, watching the fuss and thinking that I easily could have been killed in this train yard.

Trahan had finally called the Emergency Service Unit, the NYPD's SWAT guys, and a wagon circle of their diesel trucks surrounded the train yard's wheelhouse. There were K-9 units, aviation hovering, a platoon of detectives and uniforms. After Mike saw me go down, he'd called in a 10–13, 'cop in dire need,' and it seemed everyone on the force, except maybe the harbor patrol, had responded.

Lieutenant Keane hopped down from the train car where Victor Ordonez was still lying and came over.

'You did real good,' he said. 'The serial number on the gun beside our dearly departed friend in there matches. It was Scott's. Just like we thought. The Ordonezes took him out.'

I shook my head and genuinely couldn't believe what had happened. In a weird way, it had actually worked out better than I could have hoped, or dreamed. Everything was going to be okay now. Despite the stalling, the omissions, the lies.

'Any sign of Mark, the pilot brother?' I asked.

'None so far,' my boss said. 'But don't worry, he'll turn up.'

'Where's Mike?' I asked.

My boss rolled his eyes.

'IAB. Rat squad practically got here before the ESU. You'd think you getting hit might make a difference to them. Those shit-shoveling assholes think you shot yourself and dumped the gun maybe.'

I kept my breathing normal, but only through intense concentration.

Meanwhile, my boss rubbed my back like a boxer's corner man before standing him back up to fight.

'Why don't you tell this kid to get you over to Jacobi before the commissioner shows up. After the hospital, go home and unplug the phone. I'll keep the sewer rats away until you catch your breath. Give me a call sometime tomorrow. You need anything right now?'

I shook my head. I couldn't even begin to think of an answer to that question.

'You did real good, kid,' my boss said before he left. 'Made us all proud.'

I sat there watching him walk away.

The department had their shooter.

Paul was probably off the hook.

Brooke and her kids would be taken care of, as they ought to be.

I watched the blue NYPD helicopter skim over the razor wire at the rail yard's fence, then sail into the bright blue sky. Out of the corner of one eye I saw the CSU camera lights pop in the glassless window of the train car.

Everything had worked out okay, hadn't it? This was the end of the mess.

So why was I crying?

Chapter Fifty-seven

It was sunny and cool the following Monday morning.

Standing at attention out on the steps of St Michael's on 41st Street in Woodside, I was glad for the warmth of my dress blues, and for the body heat coming from the officers around me.

Though there were maybe three or four thousand cops on the cordoned-off street, waiting for the arrival of Scott's hearse, the only sound was the snapping of the honor guard's flag; the only movement the billow of its bright stars and stripes.

The rattle of snare drums began at the first tolling of St Michael's bells. From around the corner of the stone church came a forty-member contingent of the NYPD Emerald Society, the bagpipes silenced, the drummers sounding a funeral march on black-draped drums.

Behind them came a seemingly endless two-by-two line of motorcycle police, their engines crackling as they rode at parade speed.

When the sleek black body of the hearse finally slid into view, you could almost hear the lumps forming in thousands of throats. Presidents don't get put in the ground with more heart-wrenching class than an NYPD cop killed in the line of duty.

The muscles in my jaw stood out as I prevented myself from shaking, moving, breaking down completely.

From the limo that pulled to a stop behind the hearse, Brooke Thayer finally appeared. She was holding her baby and her four-year-old daughter.

A member of the honor guard suddenly broke rank and leaned into the limousine with an extended hand. Then Scott's two-year-old son finally emerged, wearing a black suit.

A black suit and his father's eight-point policeman's cap.

The Mass was excruciating. Scott's mother broke down during the second reading and his sister during the eulogy.

It was even worse when Roy Khuong, Scott's oldest friend and partner, told a story about how Scott had saved his life during a gun battle. He finished it by turning from the pulpit toward the crucifix and saying with a simple yet startling conviction, 'I love you, Scott.'

How I got through the rest of it, I'm not sure. People can survive amazing things. Look at that hiker who cut off his own arm with a pocketknife when it got stuck under a boulder. We are capable of anything, aren't we?

Well, I am. I know I am now.

They buried Scott in Calvary Cemetery on a high hill over-looking an unobstructed Manhattan skyline.

The mayor of New York gestured toward the city as he finished his graveside words.

'We ask that Scott do what he did so well in life. Watch over us, Scott. We will never forget your sacrifice.'

Brooke embraced me like a vise after I had dropped my rose among the hundreds that buried the casket's varnished lid. She touched the bandage on the side of my face.

'I know what you did for me,' she whispered. 'What you did for my family. I can sleep now. Thank you for that, Detective.'

I pulled the black lip of my cap even more tightly over my eyes to shield them, nodded stupidly and then moved along.

Chapter Fifty-eight

I sat alone in my car before leaving Calvary. I could see the flower-covered casket in my rearview.

When the skirl of the bagpipes started up, for a moment I again caught a heady gust of cologne and rain and grass. Felt again the holy, fevered heat of Scott's body in his bedroom. The strength of his jaw against my bare skin. I banished the forbidden thoughts like the demons they were as 'Amazing Grace' sailed up above the gravestones.

Mistake, I reminded myself.

It had all been a terrible mistake. Quick as lightning, just as deadly.

I looked out at the red-eyed police officers heading back to their cars. That I was fooling them burned like battery acid in my stomach, but I tried my best to believe it was the best thing for everyone under the circumstances.

What result could have been better? I thought. The dehumanizing, demoralizing tabloid circus that was the truth?

I stared out at the casket as Scott's son raised a hand in salute to the wobbling brim of his father's hat. Then I looked up at the stunning skyline of Manhattan, at the gravestones in the foreground like a kind of city itself.

My eyes were dry as I turned the engine over.

There was one undeniably good thing: Paul and I had been given a second chance.

PART TWO

COMPLICATIONS

Chapter Fifty-nine

It was coming up on nine the morning after Scott's funeral when the phone rang.

I lay there, hoping that Paul would pick it up. He'd been unbelievably terrific since the shooting. He'd even taken time off work and was cooking for me, fielding my calls, and listening when I needed to talk. He seemed to relish his role as my protector and healer. There were no more naked Scotch binges in the garage, at least, so I guess the focus on me was having a positive effect.

And I have to admit, no-nonsense, capable woman that I can be, it was a relief to have someone taking care of me for a change.

The phone kept on ringing, though, and when I turned over, I saw that Paul wasn't there.

I lifted the receiver and sat up.

I thought it would be either my boss or Mike. Maybe IAB. But I was wrong on every count.

'Lauren? Hi, it's Dr Marcuse calling. I'm glad I caught you at home.'

I shuddered, waiting to hear the worst.

'Don't worry, Lauren. Relax,' Dr Marcuse said. 'The tests came back, and everything is okay.'

I sat there, relief rattling the receiver off my bandaged head.

'You're perfectly fine, Lauren,' the doctor continued. 'In fact, you're better than that. I hope you're sitting down. You're not sick, you're . . . pregnant.'

Seconds passed. A lot of them actually. Each one filled with stark silence.

'Lauren?' I heard Dr Marcuse say faintly. 'Are you still there?'

I found myself slowly falling back on to the bed. It seemed to take quite some time for my head to actually touch the pillow.

Pregnant? I thought, feeling suddenly as if I were melting.

How could that be? How could it happen now?

Paul and I had only been trying to have kids for years. After an extensive round of fertility specialists and tests, we learned that a pH imbalance was producing an environment not conducive for conception. We'd tried everything short of fertility drugs, which weren't recommended because I had a family history of ovarian cancer.

'What? Are you sure?' I said. 'How?'

'I don't actually know, Lauren,' my doctor said, chuckling. 'I wasn't there. You tell me.'

My head was spinning. The whole room seemed to be. I'd always wanted to have a baby, of course.

But now?

'I'm pregnant?' I said, stunned, into the phone.

'You're what?' Paul said. He was just coming into the bedroom with a breakfast tray.

My mouth refused to work, so I handed him the phone. I didn't know how he'd react. I'd stopped trying to anticipate Paul's feelings. I stared into his eyes. But I didn't have to wait long. After a brief moment, a look of ecstatic surprise lit up his face, followed by an ear-to-ear grin.

'You're . . . Oh my God . . .' he said. Then he dropped the phone and lifted me out of the bed. For what seemed like an eternity, he hugged me.

'Oh God,' Paul said. 'Thank you, God. Thank you, God. This is so great.'

As we embraced, I did some quick mental math. The last time I had my period. What was I thinking? Of course it was Paul's. I'd only slept with Scott the one time, and that had been only six days ago.

Something cold inside me began to change then. The whole time I'd been convalescing, not an hour had gone by when I hadn't been attacked with feelings of guilt and shame and black anxiety.

But standing there, being waltzed around my bedroom by my joyous, good-looking husband, I suddenly came to realize something startling. Paul and I had simply tried to have what everyone wanted. A happy marriage, a happy family. We were good people, hardworking, humble. But from day one, we'd been faced with hardship. Stasis. We were two people who, try as they would, couldn't become three.

Did we divorce? Part ways because it was inconvenient to be together? No. We clung to each other, tried to make it work. For years, we struggled to make our love conquer some biological gyp. We spent years trying to keep things together while our separate careers and the everyday stresses of modern life did everything in their power to wrench us apart.

I started crying when Paul cupped my stomach with his palm. A baby! I thought, grasping Paul's hand.

A sign of hope finally.

And forgiveness.

A new life for both of us.

We can get through this after all, I thought. We really can get through this.

'I love you, Paul,' I said. 'You're going to make an amazing father.'

'I love you too,' Paul whispered, and he kissed away the tears on my cheeks. *'Mommy.'*

Chapter Sixty

There were two men sitting in my boss's office when I finally came back to work the following Monday. From the other side of the squad room, I took in their executive-looking haircuts, their dark suits.

My paranoid brain went to work instantly. Scott had worked with the DEA, which was a section in the Department of Justice. The FBI did the legwork for the DOJ. This was all I needed now, a visit from the Feds!

I didn't even make it as far as my desk before Lieutenant Keane opened his door.

'Lauren, could you come in here a second?' he said.

I brought my bodega coffee with me to make it look like I really thought this would take only a second. I was getting good at deception. At least I hoped I was.

'Have a seat, Detective Stillwell,' a man in a navy suit said from one of my boss's chairs. His partner, wearing what looked like the same style three-button, only in gray, stood at his shoulder, staring at me expressionless, motionless.

Their authoritative attitude both irritated and scared the living hell out of me. And since showing fear wasn't an option at this juncture, I tried pissed-off on for size.

'What's the dealio, Boss?' I said to Keane. 'You set me up on a blind date? Where's bachelor number three?'

Two badges came out. My adrenaline shifted down half a gear when I saw that they weren't the tiny gold badges the Feebs sport. They were copies of the one in the Chanel knock-off on my desk.

'IAB,' Navy and Gray said in unison.

So, they weren't Feds here to arrest me, I realized. My relief was short-lived when I considered that they were definitely tin-collectors here about Mike's shooting. It was too late to play demure, I realized as I sat down. Never take a step back, my father advised me when I'd decided to get on The Job after law school. He'd also given me another tidbit of wisdom.

Fuck the IAB.

'Hey, nice. Synchronized rats,' I said, plopping down in the guest chair. 'You guys should try out for the Special Olympics.'

They glared at me. I glared back.

Keane's pale face turned scarlet as he struggled to not spontaneously combust with laughter.

'That's very funny, Detective,' Navy said with a click of his pen. 'What's less funny, I guess, is the shooting death of Victor Ordonez. As we speak, there is a rally being planned in his Washington Heights neighborhood. The cry for the details of his death has gotten loud enough to be heard way down at One Police Plaza. We fully intend to find and report the truth of what occurred.'

I stared at him for a beat after his little speech.

'I'm sorry,' I said, cupping the bandage on my ear and cheek. 'Did you say something? I can't hear very well. Some virus named Victor Ordonez shot me a week ago.'

'You're coming close to insubordination, Detective Stillwell,' Gray said. 'We are here to do a routine interview. If you want us to swivel the focus of our investigation on to you, that can be arranged.'

'Swivel it off who?' I said. 'My partner? Well, get ready to write this down. My partner saved my life. I was running between two parked trains, and I was shot. I climbed for safety into one of the cars. As Victor Ordonez was attempting to come into the car where I was hiding – to finish me off, no doubt – my partner arrived and took him down.'

'How many shots were fired?' Gray said. 'Was it *boom-boom-boom* or just *boom?*'

I took a sip of my coffee and set it down on my boss's desk. Some coffee spilled and I didn't give a shit.

'It was a gunfight in a train yard,' I said. 'I was shot. I was sucking floor. I wasn't playing sound engineer for some episode of *Law and Order.*'

Gray finally slammed his book shut.

'Fine,' he said. 'But for the record, will you answer me just one more question? Detective, you were the primary investigator in this case. You were on your way to apprehend two very dangerous suspects who you believed to be responsible for the death of Detective Thayer. Why didn't you call for the tactical assistance of the Emergency Service Unit?'

I sat there for a couple of seconds. He had me on that one. It was standard operating procedure, and I hadn't done it.

I opened my mouth to say . . . God only knew what.

Then my jaw dropped as my boss jumped in.

'I authorized her to go ahead.'

I looked over at Keane. He looked back with an expression that said, keep your mouth shut.

'I determined that there wasn't enough time to wait, so I gave the go-ahead,' Keane went on. Then he rose from his seat. He walked the length of the room and opened the door for Navy and Gray.

'Now, my detective has to get back to work,' he said.

'Thanks for the save there, bossman,' I said after the IAB creeps left and Keane had shut the door again.

'Yeah, well, you and your partner are heroes as far as I and every self-respecting cop in this department is concerned,' Keane said, taking his seat back.

'And oh yeah,' he said. 'Fuck the IAB.'

Chapter Sixty-one

I was coming out of Keane's office when my partner called me on my cell phone.

'Have the rodents left the building?' Mike wanted to know.

'The two-footed ones at least,' I said.

'Come meet me for an early lunch at the Piper's,' Mike said. 'My treat.'

It took me twenty minutes or so to drive to the Piper's Kilt on 231st Street in Kingsbridge. The Bronx cop and district attorney hangout was much more bar than grill, but the burgers were outrageous. Ten thirty being on the early side, the restaurant part of the establishment was empty – except for my partner tucked away in the farthest corner booth.

After I sat, I clicked my waiting Diet Coke to my partner's Heineken.

'How's the face?' Mike said.

'Flesh wound, like you said, amigo,' I said with a shrug. 'No hearing loss either. And as a bonus, I get to wear this attractive bandage.'

Mike smiled.

'What do you think IAB will say on their report?'

'I don't know,' I said. 'I was too busy screwing with them to

get any kind of realistic gauge. Worst case, I'll probably get a repri-
mand for not following proper procedure with the ESU. I can't
see the commissioner coming down too hard on us, considering
how expedient we were in clearing this mess up for him.'

'That's true,' Mike said. 'I forgot about that.'

The waitress delivered our cheeseburgers, the buns soaked with
grease.

'Bacon too?' I said, smiling at my plate. 'Mike, you shouldn't
have.'

'Hey, for you, partner,' Mike said, lifting his bottle, 'I go that
extra mile.'

'I want to thank you, Mike,' I said after a few chomps of burger
heaven. I don't know if it was my pregnancy or what, but I was
suddenly famished. I hadn't tasted food this intensely since I'd
quit smoking eight months ago.

'I don't remember if I did or not,' I said as I popped an
escaping morsel of bacon into my mouth. 'Thanks for saving
me out there.'

'Please,' Mike said, tipping his bottle in my direction. 'I watch
your back, you watch mine. As far as I'm concerned, the police
department consists of me and you. We're like that commer-
cial for Vegas. What happens here stays here. Which reminds
me.'

Mike put down his beer and lifted up some papers from the
seat beside him.

Even in the dim bar light, I could see they were printouts. The
burger I was chewing seemed to transform itself instantly into
ketchup-flavored matchsticks as I spotted the rows and columns
of numbers.

'I found this in the fax machine yesterday,' Mike said. 'Phone
company sent over a second copy of Scott's Local Usage Details
for some reason. How do you like that? It looks just like the one

that you put on my desk, except this copy has your phone number all over it.'

Across the scarred table, Mike drank in his beer, and my complete astonishment.

'It's time to talk to me, partner,' he said. 'It's time to unburden your soul to Father Mike.'

Chapter Sixty-two

'Lauren, c'mon,' Mike whispered to me as I sat there numb and speechless. 'You didn't think you could get one over on me, did you? I mean, you're good, better than good, at what we do, but we're talking about *me* here.'

I held my Diet Coke up to my suddenly hot forehead. My God, what was I going to do now? I was busted. Busted lying to my partner. How could I have done that to him? Mike had a heart bigger than most continents. And he was my partner, my lifeline, my guardian angel on the street.

I looked down at the surface of the table, then at the dark-paneled walls of the bar, anywhere but my partner's face.

He was right, though. I had to confess. If there was anyone who I could – and should – spill my guts to, it was him. I had lied by omission and every other way, and he had killed a man because of it. Full disclosure was the least I could do for Mike.

But wait a second, I thought. No! I couldn't. If Mike got jammed up with IAB, he'd roll on me. He'd have to. He couldn't lose his job. He was divorced, but he had two kids in college. He would have to tell what he knew, and the rest of the truth would come out too. We'd be back to square one. Paul going to prison and Brooke without any means of support. No, I thought. It would actually be even worse now. I'd probably be going to jail along with Paul!

The last thing I wanted to do to my partner was be cruel – but I didn't see any alternative as I tried to think things through.

Finally I pulled my eyes down from the gin mill's tin ceiling and smacked them into Mike's head-on.

'Leave it alone, partner,' I said.

Mike made a face like I'd just shot him with a Taser. I thought the trembling, green bottle in his big hand was going to explode. For a few moments his mouth worked silently, like a clubbed fish's.

'L-l-leave it alone?' he stammered finally. 'You were sleeping with him, weren't you, Lauren? You were cheating with Scott Thayer, was that it? Why didn't you just tell me? I'm your partner, your friend.'

'Mike,' I begged him with tears forming in my eyes, 'please leave it alone.'

'I killed a man, Lauren!' Mike's whisper screamed at me. 'There's blood on my hands.'

I stood, lifted my bag.

I didn't want to threaten my partner, but I was backed into a corner. There was no other way.

'Yes there is, Mike,' I said, dropping a twenty on my uneaten fries. 'You did kill a man. I was the only witness, remember? That's why you of all people have to leave it alone.'

Chapter Sixty-three

On my way home, I called Keane and told him I felt dizzy and that I was taking a sick day. As I hung up, I realized it was one of the first times in a while I'd actually told him the truth.

I felt like I was stepping into a crypt when I opened the front door of my empty house. I decided to go for a jog and suited up. I drove to Tibbetts Brook Park five minutes away and did my usual two laps around the lake with its art-deco pool house. Jeez, it was a beautiful afternoon. Bright, yet cool. Perfect for a run. I even spotted a crane standing among the shoreline cattails as I was doing my stretches.

But by the time I sat down afterward, sweating, behind the wheel of my Mini in the parking lot, I felt like crap all over again.

Back home, I checked my empty answering machine, then poured myself a glass of wine to calm my shot nerves. Then I remembered the baby on board. The glass slipped from my shaking hand as I was pouring it back into the bottle and shattered into a thousand pieces.

Nice move, Detective, I thought as I gripped the cold edge of the sink. I was really on top of things lately, wasn't I? Really holding things together nicely.

Looking down at the glass slivers, I wondered exactly how I could have been so horrible to my partner. Flat-out threatening Mike? Who was that cold-hearted bitch at the Piper's Kilt? It sure wasn't me.

And how could I keep on doing this? I'd gone from omitting the truth, to outright lying, to threatening my friends. I didn't even want to think about what could happen next.

To top it all off, I was completely alone in all this. It was insane. I couldn't even share with Paul the stress of trying to save Paul.

This was it, I realized. Everyone has a breaking point, and I'd just arrived at mine. I couldn't keep up the 24/7 deception anymore. Lincoln was right: you couldn't fool all of the people all of the time. Not if you were Catholic, anyway.

I needed to rejoin the human race. I'd been a secret agent in my own life for long enough. This spy had to come in from the cold.

Step one was confessing my sins and unburdening myself. But not to my partner.

I had to tell Paul.

Admitting I had cheated would be excruciating, but in order to have a shot at getting ourselves and our marriage to the other side of this, Paul and I needed to be on the same page. I had to tell him that I knew what he did at the St Regis, and that I forgave him for it. And that I needed his help to make sure our dangerous secret stayed a secret.

Chapter Sixty-four

I was pulling my famous lime-cumin chicken out of the oven when Paul came in that night. With the possibility that this might be our last meal together, the least I could do was make it Paul's favorite.

My breath caught as he rushed across the kitchen and hugged me right off my feet again.

Now or never, Lauren, I thought. Time to own up.

'Paul,' I said. 'We have to talk.'

'Wait,' he said, taking a glossy folder out of his briefcase and slapping it on to the countertop. 'Me first.'

On its cover was a photograph of some very pretty rolling hills covered with bright autumn trees. Inside were the floor plans of a variety of rather large houses. It was the sales folder for a luxury housing development somewhere in Connecticut.

What the . . . ? Was he drinking again? I didn't smell any Scotch on him.

'What's this?' I said.

Paul spread out five different plans on the kitchen island with the solemnity of a fortune-teller laying out Tarot cards.

'Take your pick, Lauren,' he said. 'Pick out your dream house. Which one do you love? Personally, I love them all.'

'Paul, listen,' I said. 'Now's not the time to fantasy-shop, okay? We—'

Paul put his finger to my lips.

'I'm not kidding, Lauren,' he said. He rubbed his hands together briskly. 'You don't understand. It's not a joke, not a fantasy. I stepped in it. You ready for this? Another firm, a hedge fund, wants to steal me away for more money. A lot more money.'

'What?' I said, looking at him, then glancing at the folder again.

And then it happened. My eyes caught the heading on one of the pieces of paper in the sales folder.

Astor Court, it said. And, underneath it, *St Regis Hotel.*

The St Regis? Wasn't that . . . ? That was where I had tailed Paul and his little blonde! What was this all about?

I pulled out the sheet of paper. Numbers were written on it in a neat feminine script.

'What's this, Paul?' I asked. 'This isn't your handwriting, is it?' I expected him to suddenly turn nervous, but he glanced down at the paper nonchalantly.

'That's the initial offer from the hedge fund, Brennan Brace. Vicky Swanson, their recruiting VP, made it to me over lunch at Astor Court at the St Regis, like three, four weeks ago,' Paul said, smiling at me.

For a while, all I could do was blink.

Lunch at the St Regis?

'Vicky Swanson?' I said, vividly remembering the woman I'd seen when I went down to surprise Paul. 'What does she look like?'

'Blonde,' Paul said. 'Late twenties, I guess. Kind of tall.'

Oh God, I thought.

No! It couldn't be.

Another twist to this unending nightmare.

Lunch at the St Regis!

Paul hadn't cheated!
I gasped, struggling not to throw up.
Just me!

Chapter Sixty-five

I stood there in stunned silence.

Paul hadn't ruined everything.

It was me. I had.

Just little old me. I was the one.

Talk about putting a hitch in my dinner plans. I'd been preparing to dredge up our affairs in order to get Paul and me past them.

Except I was the only one who'd had an affair!

I stayed standing, dazed, my face frozen like the screen of a computer in safe mode. Paul laughed as he squeezed my hand.

'It's a bombshell, I know,' he said. 'I just love you, okay? See, I actually thought Vicky was bullshitting me. "Hey, would you like to come work at twice your salary?" she said. So what your brilliant husband did, as a lark really, was say that if they tripled it, they had themselves a deal.

'Vicky called me this morning with the good news. It's all approved, pending the paperwork! The only problem is, we have to move. To Greenridge, Connecticut! As if moving out of Yonkers to blue-blood horse country is a problem. They're even going to relocate us. Sell our place and give us a low-interest mortgage on our new one. This is it. Imagine! One person working, a baby, a new house with enough room for a nursery. The American

Dream on steroids. This is the break we've been waiting for, Lauren.'

My head was spinning like a blender on ice crush. I couldn't believe it. Not only was I the only one to have cheated . . .

But we'd just hit Lotto?

I sank on to my stool like a boxer after a very bad round.

'I love it, Lauren – I've actually robbed you of the power of speech,' Paul said with a laugh.

'Wait,' he said, taking a Sam Adams out of the fridge. 'Didn't you say you wanted to talk to me about something?'

I might have been on the verge of simultaneous heart and brain failure, but I wasn't stupid.

I'd learn to live with the secret of my affair somehow, I decided. Especially since I'd just found out that I was the only one who had actually had one.

'Oh, right,' I managed to mumble. 'Do you want rice or stuffing?'

Chapter Sixty-six

P aul and I made love that night for the first time since I got pregnant. I'd clicked into deep-cleaning survival mode due to his latest revelations and was folding some laundry, when I spotted a black teddie that I'd tried to seduce Paul with one afternoon before everything crazy started.

Before I knew what I was doing, I was taking off my jeans and slipping into the best of Victoria's Secret. There wasn't even any cringing mental debate when I saw the sexy version of myself in the bathroom mirror. My breasts were already larger – oh, goody!

From the suddenly stunned look on Paul's face when I came into the bedroom, I gathered he thought so too. The *Wall Street Journal* he was reading dropped from his fingers sheet by sheet until he was holding nothing but air.

'Well, well. Looks like you're going to score twice in one day, cowboy,' I said as I ripped the top sheet off the bed, sending the financial pages flying. That was pretty much the extent of our foreplay.

I don't know what had gotten into me. Could I blame my hormones? Why not? I was demanding and very specific in bed. At first, Paul looked a little shocked. Not that he didn't comply with every command. Obedient and shocked.

I felt something primal take hold of me, and I let it. Isn't that one of the big points of sex? We tear off our clothes, our inhibitions, the trappings that society demands. Thousands of years of civilization – what's right, what's wrong – are all tossed out the window and we're back to square one. Sex is the truth under all the lies. We are alive! it screams.

Right before the grand culmination, and it *was* grand, I opened my eyes and stared at Paul's handsome face above me. I looked into the steely blue of his shining eyes and suddenly I knew.

It was official.

We'd won each other back.

Chapter Sixty-seven

'My God, Lauren,' Paul said, pulsing like a lightning bug beside me afterward. 'What got into you? And your boobs?'

'I know,' I said, punching him playfully on the chest. 'Now tell me that joke again about you tripling your salary.'

'The real joke of it is that it's not a joke,' Paul said as he stared up at the ceiling. 'How about that? One day you're hopelessly stuck in the rat race. And then the next, *pow!* Your ship has come in. Make that a couple of ships.'

He rolled over and kissed my stomach.

'Hey, wait. We haven't thought about a name. Any suggestions?' I said.

'Emmeline,' Paul said. 'A little House of Windsor, I know, but if she looks half as regal as her mom, she's going to need a name that fits. Besides, she has to get a leg up on the competition at Greenridge pre-K.'

'My, my,' I said. 'Sounds like you've been thinking about this. But it could be a boy.'

'Hmm,' Paul said. 'Let's see. Melvin has a certain ring to it, don't you think? I've always been partial to Cornelius. Call him "Corny" for short.'

I tickled Paul under his arms until he sat up. 'You're the one who's corny, buster.'

'Hey, I just thought of the coolest thing this windfall is going to do for us,' he said.

'We can up our anytime minutes? We'll be able to wax now at the car wash?' I said and grinned. *This* was the way Paul and I used to be – silly.

'Very funny, Lauren,' Paul said. 'I'm serious. You can finally quit that screwed-up job of yours.'

I stared at him. Paul had always been supportive of my career. Was he serious?

'I know how important being a cop is to you, and I've never said this before,' he said. 'But c'mon. The hours. The smell of death. Do you have any idea how you look when you come home some-times? God, I hate it. I've always hated it, actually. It takes too much out of you.'

I stared into space, remembering the recent confrontation I'd had with Mike Ortiz. Maybe Paul was right. I loved my job, but family was more important. I'd certainly proved that during the past week.

'Maybe you're right,' I finally said. 'This is what we've always dreamed about. You and me and our baby together. Now it's here. It's just . . . wow. It feels surreal. Don't you think?'

'You're my world,' Paul said, tears starting in his eyes. 'You always have been, Lauren. This job offer – it's just an offer. I'll do whatever you want. Go. Stay. I'll quit my job, if you want.'

'Oh Paul,' I said, wiping his eyes. 'Our ship really has come in, hasn't it?'

Chapter Sixty-eight

Mike's desk was empty when I came into the squad room the next morning. When I asked my boss where Mike was, he reminded me of the mandatory two-week leave for officers involved in a shooting.

As I sat down, I felt another stab of guilt about what I had said to Mike. How do you like that? Mike was traumatized, extremely psychologically and emotionally vulnerable, and I had gone and threatened him. Some partner I was. Some friend.

I rocked back in my chair, looking around at the sallow walls of the squad room. So I was actually going to leave. It almost seemed crazy, after all the work I'd done to get here. I remembered how intimidated I'd been when I finally received the assignment. Bronx Homicide was one of the busiest and most renowned squads in the world, and I was unsure about what I could contribute.

But I'd done it. It had taken a lot of hard work, guts, and straight As in college Spanish to make a place for myself here, and I'd managed to pull it off.

But everything I'd accomplished was pretty much gone now, I knew. As I sat there, I could feel it. Or *couldn't* feel it, actually. What sustains you as a cop is the pure joy of being one of the good guys. That's where the movies usually get it wrong. Most cops I knew were good people. The best.

But with everything that had happened, I'd squandered that feeling. Good guys don't cheat. Good guys don't lie.

Paul was right, I thought, turning on my computer.

I was a stranger here now. I didn't belong anymore.

It was time to get out, before something else happened.

Chapter Sixty-nine

I brought up Scott's file and, for the better part of an hour, went over all the reports I'd written, every one. Then I planned to go over them again.

The news of my pregnancy and Paul's good fortune would cover the reason behind my early retirement, but some cynical eyebrows would still be raised. Definitely the IAB's. Before I made things official, I needed to make triple sure I'd covered my ass. Not to mention my tracks. And Paul's.

I was forty minutes into the paperwork when Lieutenant Keane came out of his office, carrying a set of bolt cutters and a cardboard box. He dropped them both loudly on my desk.

'I just got a call from the deputy chief's office,' he said. 'Scott's wife, Brooke, requested that someone clean out Scott's locker and bring his stuff by her house. You're elected.'

Yeah, like I really wanted to see Brooke Thayer again. Wallow a little more in the devastation I'd helped cause that family.

'What about the guys on his task force?' I said. 'Wouldn't his partner, Roy, like to do it?'

Keane shook his head.

'How about you, boss?' I said. 'Maybe it would be good for you to get out of the office. Get some sun.'

Keane tilted his stoic Irish brow at me.

'As nice as it is of you to think about my well-being,' he said, 'Scott's wife asked specifically for you.'

I nodded my head. Of course she had. I didn't really think I'd get off that easy, did I?

'How's this? You get that done and take the rest of the day,' my boss said. 'I think you came back too early anyway. If you want my opinion. Who knows when your IAB buddies might come back? I was you, I'd milk the dizzy thing for at least another week.'

'Aye, aye, bossman,' I said, saluting him as I stood.

I didn't know why, but I was going to miss Keane.

The second-floor DETF offices were, thankfully, empty. Good, I thought, going back into the locker room and snipping through Scott's Master Lock with the cutters. I was starting to realize why cops made people nervous. Guilty people, especially.

There wasn't much in Scott's locker. I removed a spare uniform, a couple of cardboard boxes of .38 rounds, a Kevlar vest. Behind a dusty riot baton, I found a fancy bottle of cologne, Le Male by Jean Paul Gaultier.

I looked over my shoulder to make sure I was still alone before I dabbed some on my wrist. There was a bang as I dizzily head-butted the door. Yep. It was the same stuff Scott had worn that night with me.

I was lifting out a pair of dress shoes from the floor of the locker when I spotted a fat envelope underneath them. Oh, Jesus!

I'm not kidding, I dropped the black shoes as if they were burning coals.

I didn't want to look in the envelope, but I knew I had to.

I opened the flap with a pencil. It was money, just as I'd suspected. A lot of it. Four or five fat rubber-banded knots of worn bills. Mostly hundreds and fifties, but there was also an impressive number of twenties and tens.

Ten, maybe fifteen thousand dollars, I thought as a migraine exploded above my left eye.

Let's see, I thought. How does fifteen grand get into a Narcotics cop's personal locker? Scott didn't trust banks? The tooth fairy was making precinct rounds?

Or, more likely, he was bad.

Scott was a bad cop, wasn't he?

'Scott,' I whispered as I stared at the dirty green crumpled edges of the bills. 'Who in God's name were you?'

What was I supposed to do now? Hand it in to my boss? Scott's case was all but closed. Did I really need the lid popping back open? Then I realized the solution was simple.

I tucked the envelope into the right shoe as far as it would go and dropped the shoes into the box.

If Brooke wanted to open up that can of worms, so be it, I thought, slamming the locker shut. It was up to her, not me.

Bringing ugly truths to the forefront was definitely not in my job description anymore.

Chapter Seventy

It took me almost an hour in bumper-to-bumper traffic to get out to Brooke's house in Sunnyside.

I left my unmarked police car double-parked as I trotted to the front door with Scott's work possessions. This visit definitely wouldn't be sweet, but I was determined to make it as short as humanly possible. After I rang the doorbell, I noticed a child's chalk drawing of an American flag on the driveway. I rang the doorbell a second time.

It took me another three minutes of ringing to decide nobody was home. I was tempted to leave the box at the back door with a note, but I couldn't be cruel to Brooke. I'd decided to head back to my Impala for a little sit-and-wait, when I heard something muffled and indistinct.

It was coming from inside the house near the door. I finally identified the noise. Sobs. Somebody was crying in there. *Oh God, not this.*

I knocked on the door this time.

'Brooke?' I called out. 'It's Lauren Stillwell. I'm here with Scott's things. Are you all right?'

The weeping only increased in volume. So I turned the knob and let myself in.

Brooke was on the stairs, curled up into herself. She looked like she was in shock. Her eyes were open, but her face was expressionless. Tears were running down her cheeks.

I panicked for a second. Had she hurt herself? I looked around for an empty pill bottle. At least there wasn't any blood.

'Brooke?' I said. 'What is it? What's going on? It's Detective Stillwell. Can you talk to me?'

I kind of patted her tentatively at first, but after a minute of the muted sobbing, I put down Scott's box and hugged her tightly.

'There. C'mon. It's going to be okay,' I said. It wasn't, but what else could I say?

The house, I could see, was messy on a level only toddlers could achieve. The toy-strewn living room looked like a page out of an I Spy book. I knelt down on the floor. *I spy with my little eye a woman in the midst of a complete nervous breakdown*, I thought.

It took another couple of minutes for Brooke to snap out of it. She finally took a deep breath that probably relieved me more than it did her. I went and found a box of tissues in the pantry.

'I'm sorry,' Brooke finally said, taking one. 'I was napping on the couch. I woke up when you pulled in, and then I looked out and saw you holding his things and . . . it was like it was happening all over again.'

'I can't imagine your pain,' I said after a pause.

Brooke's tangled blond hair fell in her face as she bowed her head.

'I don't . . . I don't know how I'm going to do this,' she said, beginning to cry again. 'My mom took the kids, and I still can't function. I can't leave the house, answer the phone. I thought the panic attacks would stop after the funeral, but they seem worse now.'

I struggled for something to say, something that might help her. 'Have you looked into group therapy?' I tried.

'I can't get into all that,' Brooke said. 'My mother-in-law and stepmom help with the kids so much as it is, and—'

'I'm not a psychologist, Brooke,' I said. 'But maybe you need to be with people like you who have lost a spouse. Nobody else can understand what you're going through. How could they? And don't worry about leaning on people in order to get better, honey. You're a parent. You have to heal yourself in order to be there for your kids.'

I don't know if Brooke bought my little pep talk, but at least she'd stopped crying and her eyes were focused.

'Is that what you would do?' she said. Her desperate gaze seized me, pinned me to the wall. 'Please tell me what to do. You're the only one in this whole thing who seems to remotely understand.'

I swallowed the lump in my throat. Brooke Thayer was looking to me for guidance? How could I go on and on fooling this woman? How could I just stand there, continuing to keep my mouth closed about what had really happened? What was I made of? Talk about scraping the bottom.

'I'd get the therapy, Brooke,' I said.

Who are you kidding? I thought. You're the one who needs therapy.

Brooke glanced at the cardboard box I'd brought.

'Could you take those things downstairs into Scotty's office for me?' she said. 'I haven't been able to go in there yet. I can't deal with all that now. I'm going to put some coffee on. Will you have some with me, Detective?'

I wanted to say no. With a bullhorn. Brooke and I were the last two females on Earth who needed to bond. But like any red-blooded American woman given the choice between her sensible desires and a guilt-laced obligation, I, of course, agreed.

'That would be really great. I could use some coffee. And please, my name is Lauren.'

Chapter Seventy-one

I blinked as I made my way down the Thayers' creaky, musty basement stairs. Wasn't the point of love affairs to have no strings attached? I had to get out of here before I was put in charge of sorting Scott's grammar school pictures, and then his underwear drawer.

I walked past a water heater and the laundry room and finally opened a plywood door covered with a Giants poster featuring Michael Strahan.

I stood still on the threshold when I turned on the light.

After the dark, oily-smelling outer basement, I was expecting to enter a typically male basement office. Tools scattered on a plywood desk. Maybe a dot-matrix printer on top of piles of *Sports Illustrated* in the corner.

So when I feasted my eyes on what looked like Don Corleone's office from *The Godfather,* I have to admit, I was a little surprised.

The walls were paneled in dark-stained oak. The antique mahogany desk looked like something made from an old ship. On top of it sat an Apple PowerBook.

There was a black leather couch and, on the wall to my right, a 42-inch Plasma TV. On top of a low bookshelf behind the desk, I counted three cell phones and a BlackBerry busily charging.

Oh brother, I thought, dread plunging through my nervous system as I put down the box beside the laptop. First the money in Scott's locker, now this fancy hideaway in the basement of his house.

I'd chosen a real multifaceted guy to sleep with, hadn't I?

Maybe between stuffing dirty money under his footwear and sleeping with married cops, Scott was Batman.

I sank into the leather office chair and closed my eyes for a few seconds. Discovering Scott's executive den made me more than a little concerned. Could he have made an itinerary of where he was heading the night he was killed? In my mind, I pictured a leather-bound calendar book with *Lauren 11 p.m.* written right under the date of his death. Stranger things had happened in homicide cases.

I hastily looked through the laptop, BlackBerry, and cell phones but, thankfully, didn't find my name or number anywhere.

After I was done, I noticed a file cabinet and an armoire-size metal locker standing in the left-hand corner of the room.

I listened for Brooke's footsteps on the stairs as I stepped toward them.

Both, of course, were locked.

I tossed Scott's desk before I found a tiny keyring among the contents of the pencil holder. The key opened the cabinet but not the locker.

My sweaty fingers nearly slipped off the handle as I rolled open the first heavy drawer.

I was partially relieved when I saw that the files looked like typical home office stuff. Folders marked 'Income Tax,' 'Credit Cards,' 'Car Repairs,' 'Dentist.'

'Lauren?' I heard Brooke call down from the top of the stairs. 'Are you all right?'

I hope so, I thought.

'Just a minute,' I called, riffling through more files. 'I'm almost finished, Brooke.'

I turned to leave after closing the last file drawer. But then I had to stick my hand under the top drawer of the desk, a nasty Homicide cop habit.

And found a DVD carefully taped to its underside.

Chapter Seventy-two

My heart ricocheted off my chest as I peeled the DVD away from the double-sided tape.

'INSURANCE' was written across it in blue marker.

Turning it in the fluorescent light, I found Scott's ever-increasing mysterious side really intriguing. Well, maybe *terrifying* was a more accurate description.

What kind of insurance comes in DVD form? The kind a man who keeps his life savings under his shoe might need, I answered myself.

Take it or leave it? I thought.

I slid it into my bag.

I guess I was taking it.

A white minivan was pulling to a stop outside the café-curtained kitchen window when I got to the top of the stairs.

'Oh, they're back already,' Brooke said with disappointment. 'Taylor's a real bear about transition. And to tell you the truth, I don't know how Scott's mom will react to seeing you. She's more devastated than me, if that's possible. Can we take a rain check on the coffee? Maybe it would be best if you left by the front door so she doesn't see you.'

'Of course, Brooke,' I said. She seemed to have pulled herself together enough to throw me out on my ear politely. That was some progress, I guess. Though in truth, she didn't have to tell me twice to get the hell out of there.

'And don't forget,' I called back as I hit the front door, 'find out about group therapy. Okay, Brooke?'

Wow, I thought, as I turned over the Chevy's engine. Group therapy. If that wasn't the most clichéd nonsense to bleat at somebody in real distress, I didn't know what was. Why didn't I recommend past-life regression therapy while I was at it?

The words that I could make come out of my mouth lately were just incredible. I glanced down at the pilfered DVD in my bag. Not to mention the actions I was capable of.

The squad car's tires made the asphalt bark as I dropped the transmission.

I was really getting this cold-hearted-bitch thing down pat.

And I hated every second of it.

Chapter Seventy-three

It was less than an hour later when I pulled off the Van Cortlandt Park South exit of the Major Deegan in the Bronx.

I swung a quick U-turn on to the service road for the Van Cortlandt Park Golf Course, reputed to be the oldest public golf course in the United States. I wasn't looking to improve my short game, just to get some privacy in the course's parking lot, one of the oldest NYPD patrol car hiding spots in the United States.

The CD/DVD slot on my laptop rang like a spent Glock clip as I fumbled with Scott's 'Insurance' DVD. I managed not to break it in my haste to get it started.

Maybe Scott had gotten the spelling wrong, I thought after a minute of watching the screen intently.

This wasn't insurance.

It was surveillance.

Vintage surveillance identified by the helpful *10:30 a.m., July 22* prominently displayed in the bottom right-hand corner of the screen.

The star of the film was a soft-looking middle-aged Hispanic man wearing a Hawaiian shirt and strolling along a city street, seemingly without a care in the world.

I deduced the setting was New York City when the Latino gentleman stopped to eat lunch by himself at an outdoor restaurant across from Union Square Park.

And that the subject had some expendable income as the film quickly cut to him getting out of a taxi and entering the Ralph Lauren flagship store on the corner of 72nd and Madison.

Was this guy a drug dealer? Considering the tape's source, and the fact that the camera seemed to be rolling from the side port-hole window of a van, I sure didn't think he was a Telemundo weatherman.

Next, the tape showed the man leaving the upscale clothing store, brimming with expensive-looking bags, and entering another taxi. The time in the corner flipped forward half an hour to show the subject exiting the cab and entering the grand front entrance of the Four Seasons hotel on East 57th Street. Everything was coming up first class.

Then the camera's vantage point suddenly changed from street level to the dizzying ledge of a thirty- or forty-story highrise. The camera panned forward and then down and the time in the corner read *6:10 p.m., July 22.*

It skimmed past the roof of the Four Seasons until one of the balconies on the 58th Street side of the hotel came sharply into focus.

After a few minutes more of silent surveillance, the camera panned down, down, down, to the street, and zeroed in on a homeless woman on the corner of Park.

'. . . the wages of sin, my Jesus. Oh, my Jehovah, forgive them, for they know not what they do,' came in clearly, as well as the rattle of her change-filled coffee cup.

Somebody must have turned on the shotgun microphone, I figured.

As the camera panned back up and stayed on the penthouse balcony, the ambient sounds of the city could be heard. The dull roar of traffic. A far-off siren. New York, New York.

Twenty long minutes of that riveting documentary coverage later, there was another cut. At first I thought maybe the DVD had blanked out, but then I noticed that the time in the corner had jumped forward seven hours to *1:28 a.m., July 23.*

The DVD hadn't gone blank, I realized. It had just gone from day to night.

There still wasn't much to see. For two minutes, other than the faint sheen from the streetlight on the metal railing of the balcony being observed, it was pitch black.

Then, suddenly, there was a bright flash, and the entire balcony was flooded with a strange greenish light.

The surveillance team had started filming in infrared, I realized. Those guys sure had access to some really neat toys.

Did Scott's task force think the pudgy Hispanic man was going to do a big drug deal out on his hotel balcony? Maybe they were hoping he would crack the sliding glass door, and they'd be able to overhear something?

I actually never got the chance to find out.

Because after fifteen more minutes of empty balcony in infrared, there was a very intrusive banging sound, and the camera panned upward about ten feet until it showed the hotel's roof.

A portly man in a tuxedo and a young woman hanging more out than in a gold-sequined party dress emerged from a service door next to the elevator housing. The camera closed in on them as they started kissing and groping passionately against an air-conditioning unit.

You could see the woman's mouth moving, and then there was a shriek as the shotgun mike was adjusted and she could be heard up close and personal.

'Wait a second,' she said.

Then she pulled her shimmering party dress over her head. She must have been really smashed, because it would have been easier to let it fall. Underneath, she was wearing just a G-string.

What the—? I thought, watching in shock.

Chapter Seventy-four

'Ah, that's much better,' the girl on the screen said, twirling around to show off her attributes, which were impressive, I had to admit.

She finally stopped and kissed the man hard on the mouth. She grabbed his outstretched hand and ran it down her body. 'Abracadabra! I've made my dress disappear.'

The man laughed.

'You're crazy,' he said. 'And shameless. I like that in a woman.'

'Now it's your turn,' the woman said. 'Let's see what you have to offer.'

'I don't know,' the man said skeptically. I couldn't see his face because his back was to the camera. 'All these windows. Somebody might see.'

'How? You can't even see your hand in front of your face,' the young female exhibitionist said. 'C'mon, John. Have some balls for once in your life. Have some fun!'

'I'll think about it,' the man said. 'I just have a little business to attend to first.'

Turning around, the man lowered his large head, and then there was a loud snorting sound.

'Hey, save some for me, will ya?' the woman said, coming over. 'You sound like a Piggy Wiggy.'

There was another snort.

'This shit is sweet,' the man named John said. 'Not like that other crap you brought last time. My nose was bleeding for a week. I had to tell my wife it was dry sinuses.'

'Another word about your wife,' the girl said, 'and I'll go downstairs to your room right now and wake her sorry ass up. Now, I snort and you strip.'

'What the beautiful lady wants,' the man said as he pulled off his jacket, 'the beautiful lady gets.'

I cringed, hovering the cursor over the 'fast forward' button as the man unbuckled his belt. He fell over as he was trying to pull his pants and underwear over his shoes. His pale flanks would have probably shone without the infrared as he unsuccessfully tried to right himself.

Then he turned, and the camera did a quick close-up on his face.

And I clicked on the media player's 'pause' button so hard I nearly cracked the mouse.

It was Bronx district attorney John Meade.

I sat there, trying not to hyperventilate, as the significance of everything dawned on me. I already knew Scott was a bad cop. Had he been stealing money from raids? Robbing drug dealers? Whatever. It didn't matter. He was definitely not doing what he was supposed to.

And here, on this particular surveillance, he'd stumbled upon a real, unexpected bonus.

I looked at the important lawyer, his bare sack-of-meal belly, the red eyes above his doped-up half-smile.

By accident, or maybe not, Scott had captured the one man most capable of hurting him – the district attorney for the borough where he worked and stole. In the most compromising position imaginable. Having an affair *and* doing coke.

You couldn't get this kind of backup insurance from Aflac, I thought.

I listened to the rumble of traffic on the highway behind me.

I couldn't believe it. Lies. Dirty money. Now blackmail. Scott hadn't been Batman after all. He'd been Harvey Keitel in *The Bad Lieutenant*.

The dirt just kept on coming.

I closed the lid of my laptop as I started my car.

I was in this up to my neck.

Chapter Seventy-five

The next morning, I woke up with the surprising and some-what bizarre idea that it was a good time to take a week of saved-up vacation.

And starting, Monday, that is exactly what I did. In spite of everything, I actually had a fairly good time. Instead of sex, lies, and videotape, it was sex, food, and jogging, mostly in the reverse order.

I divided my mornings and afternoons between spending quality time with the crane at Tibbetts Brook Park and learning how to cook like Julia Child again. Every night, I made sure Paul came home to a new, knock-his-socks-off homemade meal: red wine pot roast with porcini, roasted duck breast with black truf-fles, and his personal favorite, grilled dry-aged porterhouse with twice-baked potatoes.

And it wasn't just his socks that were knocked off usually. Our life in the bedroom was back on track, and maybe even better than ever. Honestly, we couldn't get enough of each other.

Hugging in the dark afterward, a kind of fugue would settle over me, and everything – the dark past, the uncertain future – would suddenly go away.

Then the ax finally fell on Thursday of my vacation week.

It came in the form of a phone call out of the blue. It was ten o'clock and I was unlacing my Reeboks when I noticed the blinking message light.

No news had meant good news for so long.

So, who was calling me at home on my vacation? I pressed the message button to find out.

'Detective Stillwell, this is assistant district attorney Jeffrey Fisher from the Bronx County Office. I know you're on vacation, but we're going to need you to come in and tie up a few loose ends on the Thayer case. Tomorrow at ten will be good for us. Bronx County Courthouse, second floor.'

I played the message over and over again.

What disturbed me the most was that I had a lot of friends in the Bronx DA's Homicide office, but I knew Fisher the least. It seemed like maybe he had drawn the short straw on a distasteful task. And what about the semicasual tone of the message? *Tie up a few loose ends* sounded like it wasn't a big deal. Which didn't really make sense when I considered the officious-sounding ordering of the where and when at the end. I'd used the same textbook-law-enforcement implication that something mandatory was voluntary in trying to get witnesses to talk to me.

Witnesses, I thought, closing my eyes.

Not to mention *suspects*.

For a moment I panicked, beginning to think about what might have happened, where I might have screwed up, what the DA might try to lay on me. But then I stopped myself.

I knew how this game was played, and I knew that even in the worst-case scenario I had the advantage. Because the fact was, even if the DA came out and accused me and Paul of murdering Scott, they still had to prove it. Which was going to be hard, since there were no fingerprints, and Paul had never mentioned to anyone what he had done. Not even to me.

You could know somebody did something and they could still walk. I knew that full well. You had to prove your case in a court of law, and you needed evidence just to get there.

Sitting by my phone, I tried to turn my fear into something useful. If the DA's office wanted to play hardball, I decided, then I would be ready for them.

My hand started trembling before I could reach the 'delete' button, though.

Yeah, right. Who was I kidding?

How the hell would I pull this one off?

Chapter Seventy-six

After a restless and unnerving night with almost zero sleep, I decided to strap my gun and badge under my favorite Armani Exchange black suit. The skirt had a side slit in it that ordinarily would disqualify it as work clothes, but this wasn't going to be a typical day at the office, was it?

I peeled off my bandage and teased my freshly razor-cut and colored hair before sliding into a pair of Steve Madden open-toed slingbacks.

My meeting at the DA's office was going to be combat, right?

I'd need every weapon I could come up with for this encounter with the law.

I gave myself plenty of time to swing by the Bronxville Starbucks for a venti. I finished it by the time I found a parking spot in Lou Gehrig Plaza across the street from the courthouse. I stared out at Yankee Stadium at the bottom of 161st Street, hoping maybe some of the Bomber mystique would rub off on me.

Unfortunately, from where I was sitting, it was looking like two outs in the bottom of the ninth.

It was nine thirty, a full half-hour before my scheduled meeting, when I located Fisher at his desk on the second floor. He was sitting with three other male assistant district attorneys.

'Hey, fellas. How's it going?' I said, staring into their eyes one by one.

I'd done all I could to look my best. From the head-swiveling of just about every male court officer, defendant, and counselor I'd passed in the marble halls, I figured that I'd cleaned up pretty well.

I popped a button on my jacket, giving the guys a peek at my Glock in the pancake holster pressed tightly against my stomach.

If this had been a cartoon, eyeballs would have been popping out and big red hearts would have been banging in and out of the lawyers' chests. A hot chick and a gun? Hard to beat. Men are nothing if not predictable.

'You have the right to remain silent, guys,' I said, 'but this is ridiculous. Don't you think?'

There were 'gotta go's' and 'see ya, Jeff's,' and one by one the lawyers moved along until it was just me and my friend Fisher in the cramped cubicle. I nearly knocked him out of his rolling chair as I slid my butt up on the side of his desk.

The key to winning any battle is to put your opponent off balance. Hit the weak spot, and don't let up until it's all over but the shouting. The one thing I remembered about Fisher, a balding, hangdog-looking thirty-something, was the way he had tried to look down my dress at a Piper's Kilt retirement party the year before.

'You said you wanted to see me, Fisher?' I said.

I watched his face flush the brightest red this side of a stop-light.

'Yes, uh, well, Detective,' the ADA stammered. 'I mean . . . uh, it's probably nothing. I'm sure it is. Where did I put that file? It'll just take a second.'

As I watched him flail around over his desk, I had the feeling I'd already won this round. Interrogations were power struggles.

Up until a moment before, with his cryptic message left on my machine, Jeffrey Fisher thought that he was in charge. But not anymore.

ADAs have a built-in inferiority complex when it comes to Homicide cops. The fact that Fisher was probably attracted to me kind of sealed the deal.

He would tread lightly. Whatever inconsistency he brought up, I would deny, and he would accept it. What had I been worrying about? I owned this meeting. Who was Fisher? Some nine-to-five schlep lawyer who was afraid to set foot on the dangerous streets of the Bronx? I would walk out of here blameless and free. I could feel it.

But then, out of nowhere, like some horrible apparition, Fisher's boss, Jeff Buslik, appeared. Buslik didn't look tongue-tied. In fact, he seemed extremely calm and collected. Malevolently calm. He didn't even seem impressed with my outfit. He kissed me chastely on the cheek like I was his sister.

'Lauren, how's it going?' he said. 'Actually, I called the meeting. Why don't we head into my office?'

Oh no, I thought.

Oh fucking no!

Chapter Seventy-seven

I followed Jeff. His office was a corner one, facing the stadium. You could see the Yankees right-field seats out the copper-rimmed window.

'Hey, you can spy on the bleacher creatures from here,' I said.

'How do you think I clear my fugitives' docket?' Jeff joked. He looked down at his desk pensively, as if searching for the right words.

'Listen, Lauren. I like you. I really do. You're a terrific cop and . . .'

'I'm married, Jeff,' I said with a grin.

'I know that. Okay. I guess I'll just come out and ask. Did you have anything to do with the death of Scott Thayer?'

There it was. The bomb blast I'd been hoping would never come. I felt deaf for a second. I could almost feel my shadow burn into the wall behind me.

As I fought to gain back my breath, I wondered if they could process me right here in the courthouse. Send me out with the other prisoners in the van to Rikers Island.

'Of course,' I said after a long beat. I was smiling to let him know I thought he was joking. 'I was the Homicide investigator in charge of his case.'

'That's not what I meant,' Jeff said quietly.

I looked into the prosecutor's eyes. What could I say now? What could I do?

Do something, a voice told me.

Fight. Or die.

'Yeah, well, what the hell *do* you mean, Jeff? What is this? Scott's case is closed. I remember because the lid almost took my head off when it slammed. Has IAB called you? Is that what this is all about?'

'Three days ago, this office was contacted by the attorney of one Mr Ignacio Morales,' Jeff said. 'He was a bouncer at the club Wonderland, where you went to apprehend the Ordonez brothers.'

Oh, crap.

'Yeah, I remember Mr Morales,' I said. 'Did Mr Morales happen to mention that he was about to rape me in the club's basement?'

Jeff held up his hand as if to swat away that minor detail.

'He claims that the gun they found on Victor Ordonez's body was removed from your handbag in a routine security search at the nightclub.'

I made my eyes bulge to project my outrage. I think Nicole Kidman would have been envious.

'And you believed this?' I said.

'Well, actually no,' Jeff said. 'I trust that drug-pushing vermin about as far as I could bench-press him.'

Jeff reached into his drawer and took out a piece of paper.

'But then I saw this.'

It was Scott's LUDs. Had my partner sent them to him? Even in my panic, I didn't believe that. Ever-efficient, never-miss-a-thing genius Jeff must have asked for his own copy.

I'd been somewhat expecting this to come up. So I came out the only way I had left to me – swinging.

'So what?' I said. 'So I knew Scott. We talked on the phone.

Our relationship was nobody's business, so I never mentioned it. There a crime in protecting my privacy?'

Instead of answering, Jeff took out another sheet of paper and pushed it across his desk.

It was a photocopy of a parking ticket for a motorcycle. It was really nice of him to allow me the time to thoroughly read the highlighted date and the address.

The Yonkers address half a block from my house.

A cathedral's worth of panic bells went off inside me.

I hadn't been expecting this one.

'That Yonkers PD ticket was scratched on Scott's illegally parked vehicle a couple of hours before the coroner's time of death,' Jeff said calmly. 'I looked up the location on a map.

'It's half a block from your house, Lauren. Talk to me here. Make all this make some sense. Because I have grand jury justification right now. A witness that saw you plant the gun. And evidence that puts Scott down the block from your house just before the ME's time of death. I've won cases with far less, Lauren. But you're a friend. I wanted to give you the benefit of the doubt before any formal proceedings. This is your first and last chance to tell me what happened, and to let me help you.'

Chapter Seventy-eight

It was tempting. I'd held back so much for so long. Had lied to my friends and colleagues.

The desire to justify myself, to relieve myself of my burden, was almost unbearable. I wanted to explain how, at first, I was just afraid, and how everything had happened so fast. How I'd only wanted to protect my husband, Paul. How I did it all for him.

Now I knew how so many of the suspects I'd put away over the years felt right before they folded, purged themselves, gave it up. Confession was the last step to forgiveness, wasn't that the con?

But then I remembered.

I didn't need forgiveness.

I had a pretty good Plan B.

I did something then that I suspected Jeff Buslik didn't see too often in his high-powered corner office. I leaned back in the hot seat across from him, folded my hands on my tight-skirt-clad lap, and smiled.

Then I swung for the fences!

'I see you have a lot of paper evidence here, Jeff,' I said. 'But I'm wondering, do you have any video evidence?'

'What?' the chief deputy DA said. There was a look on his face that I'd never witnessed before. Complete befuddlement.

'Lauren, please. Now isn't the time for nonsense, okay? I have a job to do here, and if you don't want to try to informally take a step in the right direction, I guess we'll have to—'

'*Video* evidence, Jeff,' I continued. 'Video evidence is incontrovertible, isn't it? The only reason I keep harping on it is that, in the course of my investigation, I came across a . . . well . . .'

I took my laptop out of my bag, turned it on, and hit 'play.'

'Maybe you ought to see this for yourself,' I said. 'You really should, Jeff.'

Chapter Seventy-nine

I let him watch from the beginning of the surveillance to the end, uninterrupted. I sat staring out his window at the stands in the stadium. My dad had taken me to my first game there when I was eight. I didn't catch a home run, but I did taste my first beer when a drunk behind us dropped one on my head.

I wondered what my dad would think of all this, of me. Would he be ashamed? Or proud that I was capable of getting bare-knuckle down and dirty to fight for my survival? I listened for some sign from my father as I waited. But all I heard was the number 4 train rattling by.

When he was finished watching the DVD, Jeff Buslik snapped the laptop closed and took a good long look out the window himself.

We listened to the heavy silence together for a while.

The video was of Jeff's boss, John Meade, but in a way, that was even better than if it had been of Jeff. Jeff was going to run for the DA's office next November when Meade stepped down, and word was, he was a shoo-in to win. And that wasn't the only office he would be seeking, it was rumored. Diamond-bright, black, and with real star presence, he was already being called the Barack Obama of the Bronx by the press.

But the political fact of life was, Jeff needed his boss's blessing. John Meade was a Bronx institution, and Jeff was his right-hand man. Until Election Day, at least, they were inextricably connected, and if John Meade crashed, Jeff would burn along with him.

Jeff seemed to realize this as much as I did. He looked like he had an upset stomach all of a sudden. A bad one. Finally he moved his sour gaze on to me.

'Evidence,' I repeated. 'You have it. I have it. Listen, I have no hard feelings, Jeff. I understand coming after me would be huge for you. National coverage, maybe celebrity status. I think it's great for somebody to want to get ahead. But if you take me on, I swear to God, the next time you see this footage, it'll be on the Fox News channel.'

Jeff thought about that one for a little while.

'Did you kill him, Lauren?' he finally said. 'Did you actually kill Scott Thayer?'

'No,' I said. 'Don't you read the papers? Victor Ordonez did. Anyway, I am resigning. I just can't take this crazy crap anymore. I think it's best to go out on a high note. Kind of like your boss. Don't you think that's best?'

I stood and popped the DVD out of the laptop.

'We're done here, right?' I said. 'Our friendly little chat?'

Jeff sat there silent for another minute. Then he turned, and the shredder behind his desk screamed twice, almost with glee, as he fed Scott's phone records and the parking ticket into it.

'We're done, Lauren,' Jeff said quietly to the far wall. There was a sadness in his voice. He didn't turn around again until I was gone.

'I didn't kill him,' I finally said – but only after I was outside the building, walking to my car.

PART THREE

THE WASHINGTON AFFAIR

Chapter Eighty

'**M**ore sparkling water, signora? More chianti, signore?'
'*Si,*' Paul and I said in unison. Let the good times roll,
right?

The stubbled young waiter beamed with elation as he topped
off our glasses, almost as if we'd just granted him his life's wish.
Behind him, the pale stone walls of Monticiano, the newest and
most expensive Italian restaurant in Greenridge, Connecticut,
glowed like a Tuscan sunset.

Paul's surprise dinner trip north to Litchfield County's only
four-star Italian had been more than welcome after my draining
morning at the courthouse.

After what I'd managed to pull off with Jeff Buslik, I thought,
as I took another mind-blowing bite of my fettuccine with truf-
fles, I deserved a trip to the real Tuscany.

'Signora, the signore would like to propose a toast,' Paul said.
'To the future,' he said.
'To the future.'
We clinked glasses.

And to us being safe and together once and for all, I thought,
taking a cool, clear sip of my San Pellegrino.

Paul drank his wine and leaned back, smiling. It was like he somehow sensed everything was okay now, that the craziness was over, and that our new life – our real life – was about to start.

In the flickering candlelight, I stared at Paul, almost as if for the first time. His sandy hair, his intense blue eyes, his strong hands – hands that had fought for me.

'Honey? Honey, listen,' Paul said, and he leaned across the table toward me. 'Can you believe it?'

From the speakers, Frank Sinatra was singing 'The Way You Look Tonight.'

Our wedding song.

Could it have gotten any more disgustingly perfect? My heart floated like the bubbles in my glass. That confirmed it, I decided. Paul and I would be together now. Finally happy, finally free. With the child we'd always wanted.

'Well, what do you think?' Paul asked after the song ended.

'The pasta?' I said. *'Bellissima.'*

'No,' Paul said. 'The new neighborhood.'

Greenridge might have been just another quaint New England small town, except for the pricey art galleries, the pricey wine shops, and the pricey day spas up and down Main Street. Norman Rockwell meets SoHo. Monticiano itself was housed in a repurposed nineteenth-century firehouse. I'd read in *New York* magazine that a lot of New York City fashion designers and artists had country homes here. With the second-lowest crime rate in the entire northeast, why wouldn't they?

'It's mind-boggling that we're going to move anywhere,' I said. 'But to here?'

'And you haven't even seen the house yet,' Paul said. 'The tour starts after dessert.'

A new house, I thought. I mean, a roof that didn't leak? Doors that closed and stayed closed? I shook my head with amazement.

I think it was still spinning when the waiter came back ten minutes later. 'Some cappuccino, signora? Tonight's dessert special is cannoli with a lemon cream.'

'*Si*,' I said, leaning back on my banquette, basking in my relief, the golden glow of the night, our insanely good luck. '*Si, si, si.*'

Chapter Eighty-one

Half an hour later, Paul was driving faster than he ought to have been in his Camry. My shoulder belt and stomach tensed simultaneously as he suddenly braked, and we swerved off the ridiculously bucolic road we'd been winding our way along over hill and dale.

The sign outside my window, placed at the base of a stone fence, no doubt by kind woodland creatures or perhaps Robert Frost himself, read 'Evergreens.'

In the fading light, the shadows of softly swaying pine trees along the drive printed a golden barcode across the fresh asphalt.

'What do you think?' Paul said, stopping the car.

'So far,' I said, looking around, 'so awesome.'

'You hear that?' Paul said, rolling down his window.

I listened. All I could hear was the wind rustling the leaves.

'Hear what?'

Paul smiled.

'Exactly,' he said. 'This is what it sounds like when there are no jackhammers or bus engines or raving homeless people. I've read about this somewhere. It's called peace and quiet, I think.'

'What are those grayish-looking things alongside the road – with that green stuff on top?' I said, squinting out my window.

'Those are called trees,' Paul said. 'They talk about them in the brochure. They come with the house – if you upgrade the cabinets.'

Paul restarted the car and continued on to the top of the hill, where he stopped again so I could see all the houses in our neighborhood. They were beautiful, what else? New England-style colonials, maybe a half-dozen of them, well spaced and landscaped down a rolling valley.

'Okay,' I said, 'what's the downside? Where's the catch? We're right in the landing path of an airport?'

'Sorry,' Paul said as we began making our way back down the hill. 'Greenridge has an ordinance against downsides. Besides, we've had enough downsides to last a couple of lifetimes.'

Paul didn't know the half of it.

Chapter Eighty-two

We passed an enormous playground, tennis courts, a manicured baseball field. I looked out at the precisely laid, brand-new white lines. Yep, it looked like a real neighborhood. *Leave It to Beaver*'s maybe. My head continued to spin.

The sun was almost completely gone when we stopped in front of a large house beside a park with a stream.

'What's this? The sales office?' I said.

Paul shook his head. He took out a key.

'It's the clubhouse,' he said. 'C'mon, I'll show you the lay of the land.'

Inside were conference rooms, several flat-screen TVs, a well-stocked weight room. Fliers on the bulletin board touted babysitting and block parties. There was a sign-up sheet for something called a progressive dinner at one-fifty a head.

'And they're putting in a pool in the spring,' Paul said, plopping down on a leather couch in the vaulted lobby space.

'How can . . .' I started. 'Even with your raise, this seems . . .'

'The houses are expensive, but it's pretty far from the city, so it's less than you think. My new salary will cover us and then some. You want to see our house? At least it *will* be ours – if you love it as much as I do.'

I put up my hand.

'Just give me a second to pick up my jaw first.'

There was a halo of last light over the western hills as we pulled off the paved drive on to a dirt road that was still under construction. We crawled slowly past mounds of broken rock and heavy machinery.

'I need to take it slow,' Paul said. 'There are nails and bolts scattered around from the construction. Don't want to get a flat. Wait, we're here.'

The dove-gray house Paul pulled in front of was . . . well, perfect. I took in the front porch, the soaring brick chimney, the graceful dormers on the third floor. Wait a second – there was a third floor? Everything looked done except the landscaping, which I was quite certain would be wonderful too.

'C'mon,' Paul said. 'I'll show you the master suite.'

'Are we allowed to be here? Don't we have to wait until the closing? Are you sure?'

'Sure I'm sure,' Paul said with a laugh. 'I'll leave the headlights on so we can see where we're going.'

We walked over the mounded dirt, and Paul opened the unlocked front door. Suddenly he threw me over his shoulder in a fireman's carry and pretended to trip as he brought me across the threshold. Our laughter and footsteps echoed off the gleaming hardwood floors. 'I love it already,' I whispered. 'I really love it, Paul.'

Paul showed me where everything would be. I could hardly take in the airplane-hangar-size kitchen, my eyes darting from maple to granite to stainless steel. Even in the dark, the tree-covered hills out the windows were breathtaking.

'And this is where the nursery could go,' Paul said, hugging me in one of the upstairs rooms.

Outside the 'nursery' window, stars were twinkling like diamond dust in the midnight-blue sky just above the dark treetops. My tears started flowing then. It was suddenly real. Our baby would grow up in this room. I saw myself holding a sweet-smelling, cooing bundle and pointing out the constellations, the rising moon.

Paul wiped away the tears on my face and kissed the ones on my throat.

'That bad, huh?' he whispered.

Then, as suddenly as I'd started, I stopped crying.

Because at that moment, the headlights of Paul's car, which had been lighting the house, suddenly went out.

The tears went cold on my cheeks as the house turned as black as the spaces between the stars.

Chapter Eighty-three

'What the—?' Paul said in the dark. 'Is it the battery? You have any idea, Lauren?'

I stared at him. *What the hell was going on?* Whatever it was, I didn't like it.

'Hey, wait. I know,' Paul said. 'My fault. I saw the tank was low yesterday, and I forgot to fill it. All this driving, we must have run out of gas.'

'Are you sure?' I said. I felt a little panicked, actually. Guess I wasn't really used to the country yet.

'Calm down, Lauren. This isn't the South Bronx, Detective,' Paul said, and laughed. 'I'm positive that's it. There has to be a gas can floating around here with all this construction equipment. You stay here. I'll grab the flashlight and pooch around.'

'I'll come with you,' I said. The unlit house had gone from cozy to creepy in no seconds flat.

'In those heels?' Paul said.

'Hey,' I said, regaining my senses. 'Instead of foraging for fuel, why don't you just call Triple A with your cell phone?' Or better yet, I thought, glancing down the stairs into the darkness, 911.

Paul laughed after a minute.

'That's my Lauren,' he said, going into his pocket. 'Always have to spoil a little fun with that pesky logic.'

His hand came out empty.

'I left my cell charging in the car,' he said. 'We'll have to use yours.'

'It's in my bag on my seat of the car.'

'Wait here. I'll go and grab it.'

'Be careful,' I called to Paul.

'Don't worry about me. This is Connecticut, sweetheart.'

Chapter Eighty-four

The next few minutes went by slowly. A cold wind suddenly blew into the house from the window cut-out. I stared out at the swaying trees that now looked like they belonged on the set of *The Blair Witch Project*. Ghosts couldn't haunt a new construction, could they?

I checked my watch again. Shouldn't Paul be back by now? How long did it take to get a cell phone out of the car?

I stepped toward the stairs with relief when I finally heard Paul's footsteps. He was standing on the open front-door threshold, holding a powerful flashlight. Had he gotten it from the trunk?

'You get through?' I called down.

The flashlight swung toward my face, blinding me. Then heavy footfalls pounded up the stairs.

'Quit it, Paul,' I said. 'Not funny.'

'Wrong, bitch,' a strange voice said. Then a rough hand struck my chest, and I was thrown backward to the floor.

Not funny. And *not* Paul.

For the next half-minute, I was unable to do anything. See, breathe, think, speak, make my heart beat. When I was able to concentrate again, I lifted my head up and squinted at the face of the shadowed figure who was standing with an unnerving stillness behind the blinding flashlight.

'Who are you?' I said.

'You don't know?' the voice said with disgust. 'You actually have to rack your brain to come up with a name? You are one amazing bitch.'

The flashlight suddenly shifted up to the man's face. *Oh, Jesus.* I muffled a scream – which came out as a groan instead.

My lips began trembling as I recalled his mugshot. Dark, soulless eyes above high, pock-marked cheeks.

I was looking at Mark Ordonez.

The recently deceased Victor's brother!

Where was my gun? was my next thought.

A soft, metallic click sounded beside the light. 'You left it in the car, dumbass,' the drug dealer said, reading my mind.

'Listen, this isn't the way to handle this,' I said quickly. 'Trust me, it isn't.'

Ordonez answered me by cuffing my arms behind my back. 'Get up!' he snarled.

I stood, feeling strange and powerless. I felt like I was weightless as the drug dealer forced me down the stairs, holding the back of my collar.

'Check this out,' Ordonez said as we stepped outside on to the loose dirt of the front yard.

He flashed his light on a form lying beside our car.

The image came to me spottily, as if through TV white snow. It was Paul, faceup, his body almost completely under our car. Blood pooled on the ground beneath his head. He wasn't moving at all.

'Oh God!' I said, dropping on my knees. 'Oh no! No! Paul!'

My mouth dried instantly as Ordonez yanked me up and dragged me around one of the mounds of earth, and I saw the van. Its side door slid open wide, an open doorway leading to blackness.

The only sound now was from our feet crunching gravel.

I lost one of my shoes. After I hobbled for a moment, Ordonez stopped, stooped, and yanked off my other one. He heaved it away into the darkness.

'You won't need it,' he said. 'Trust me on that.'

Down the hill behind the van, I watched a window light go on in one of the distant houses. I pictured a family sitting down at a dining room table, kids laying out plates and silverware, Dad loosening his tie. The countless stars above the houses twinkled.

Not for you, I thought, as I was thrown into the van's open doorway.

The cold metal floor slapped against my cheek, and then there was just blackness and the *slide-bang* of the door shutting. The metallic noise echoed in my ears.

It was the sound of the world slamming its door in my face for good.

Chapter Eighty-five

I couldn't stop picturing Paul's body lying in the dirt beside his car.

It took me a full ten minutes to stop shivering and to finally recover my ability to speak.

'Where are you taking me?' I said, turning toward the front of the van.

Mark Ordonez was fiddling with a silver gadget on the van's dashboard as he drove. Music suddenly filled the van. Old music with a lot of horns. It sounded absurd under the circumstances.

'You like XM?' he called back to me. 'This oldie's "Fly Me to the Moon." Frank's Place shit is the mack daddy.'

He rolled his neck. With his military-style flat top, he looked like an understated, more disciplined version of his brother. The only flashy object he wore was his watch, a steel Rolex. Why did he scare me even more than his brother? He had a travel mug in the drink holder by his elbow. He lifted it out and took a sip.

'Where are we going?' I asked again.

'Oh, nowhere,' he said. 'Got a Piper in an airport across the Connecticut border in Rhode Island. I thought I'd take you on a little night flight. You up for it?'

What was left of my heart sank. I wanted to cry, but to cry was to care too much about myself. The last thing I should do at this point, after all the pain and destruction I had brought to every person I was close to, was worry about myself.

A searing numbness possessed me as I thought about Paul. Dear God, I prayed. Let him be okay. I really must have been in shock – like God was taking requests from me at this point.

I lay there, silent, as we rattled along.

'Ah, screw it,' Ordonez said, lowering the radio. 'I'll tell you where we're going if you let me in on something.'

I watched as his cold gray eyes found mine in the rearview mirror.

'So tell me, why did you and your partner kill my brother, then frame him for murder? He didn't kill that cop. You know it, and so do I. I mean, what the hell? Why?'

I felt a stab of hope as we rolled along. Ordonez thought I had something he wanted. Information about his brother. I had to use that to stall him, get him off balance, create a chance to save myself.

'We got a tip from an informant,' I finally said.

'An informant?' he said. 'How convenient for you. Snitch have a name?'

'I'm sure they do, only I don't know it,' I said. 'The tip came through Scott's task force team. Somebody in your organization, I can tell you that for a fact. Give me a chance, and I'll help you find him.'

'Wow,' Ordonez said. 'You're almost as good a liar as Scotty was. He always liked sharp-minded pieces of ass like you, even back in high school.'

I craned my neck and stared, wide-eyed, at the rearview mirror. *What did he just say?*

'You and Scott were friends?' I blurted out.

'Scott was my homeboy,' the drug dealer said, rolling his eyes.

'Back in the day when me and Vic was moving nickel bags, we used to plan fake busts with Scotso. Split our boss's money. I used to tip him off about our competition, money couriers. He used to tip me off about heat coming in my direction.'

Ordonez laughed at my shocked expression.

'The night Scott ended up dead, I was supposed to meet him. Only he postponed. Told me he had a booty call from this hot little Homicide detective. Up in Yonkers. You know who that hottie was?'

I closed my eyes, gritted my teeth. I couldn't believe what an idiot I was.

'Yeah, Scott was one slick cat,' Ordonez said. 'Only I guess he ran out of lives that night with you. You ever ask yourself what angle he was playing on you? Besides getting in your pants, of course. Because he *never* did nothing without some twisted reason, believe me. My boy Scotty, he was Freddy Krueger with a badge, more twisted than a pretzel.'

We drove in silence after that little bit of wonderfulness.

'You still want me to tell you where we're headed?' Ordonez said after a minute.

I nodded. 'Yeah, I do.'

'We're going to fly due east of Providence for an hour or so. You know where that will put us?'

I shook my head. 'I don't.'

Ordonez winked at me in the mirror.

'The Atlantic Ocean,' he said. 'About a hundred and fifty miles from land. Then – pay attention now, this is good – I'm going to slice open the palms of your hands and the soles of your feet.'

My breath started to come in sobbing bursts.

'Don't worry, lady. Nothing life-threatening,' Ordonez said. 'But then I'm going to slow air speed, lower altitude, and plonk you out the door of the Piper into the deep blue sea. You getting the picture now? You feeling me?'

I suddenly couldn't get enough oxygen. If my hands hadn't been cuffed, I would have covered my ears.

'From that point, you have exactly two choices,' he continued as I experienced my first-ever asthma attack. 'Drown yourself, or try to survive. You seem like the spunky type. I'm guessing you'll think you're going to get lucky – a passing boat or plane will spot you, pick you up. Only that's *not going to happen.*'

Ordonez took a sip of his drink and adjusted his rearview mirror. He cold-eyed me. Then he winked at me again, horribly.

'While you tread water, your blood will seep. Then the sharks will come, Lauren,' he said. 'Not one, not two. I'm talking hundreds of sharks. Every hammerhead, blue, sandtiger, maybe even a great white or two, will be all over you like a bum on a bologna sandwich. And then, Lauren – I'm not kidding here, I want you to be fully informed – you're going to experience the worst death imaginable. Alone, in the middle of the ocean, you're going to be eaten alive. In case you've been wondering, I *loved* my brother, well, like a brother.'

Ordonez suddenly turned up the radio, I guess to show his total disdain for me.

What I heard couldn't be, I thought. But it was.

Frank Sinatra.

Oblivious to the irony, Ordonez checked his Rolex and took another sip from his mug.

'"Just the way you look . . ."' he sang along with ol' Blue Eyes, with a jaunty snap of his fingers, '"tonight."'

Chapter Eighty-six

For the next ten minutes or so, a kind of terror seizure overtook me. I lay facedown on the floor of the van, as still as a corpse in the back of a hearse. Mark Ordonez drove smoothly, keeping it at a steady fifty-five in order not to attract any attention.

From the occasional rumble of passing trucks, I assumed we were on I-84 heading east toward Rhode Island. How much more time until we arrived at the airport? Another hour?

Slowly, I began to come out of my fit. Just in time to realize who, in all of this, I'd hurt most of all. I turned on my side and brought my knees up until my thighs were almost touching my stomach.

Whoever you are, I told the baby in my womb as I shook with sorrow, I'm so sorry. So sorry, so sorry for you, my little one.

There was a hard shake as the van suddenly jogged sharply to the right.

'*Hey!*' Ordonez shouted, staring into his driver's-side mirror as we swerved back again.

'This guy's gotta be drunk. Pick a lane, buddy.'

A second jarring shift flipped me over on to my stomach. Immediately after that, there was a loud, crunching bang, and the driver's-side wall of the van bent inward. Jesus! What now?

A steady rumbling noise along with a violent vibration suddenly filled the van. I realized that we had driven over the grooved shoulders that are there to keep drivers from falling asleep. The sound was like a bizarre alarm clock going off inside my skull as my forehead did a drumroll on the van floor.

'Son of a bitch!' Ordonez yelled, gunning the accelerator. The van's engine roared, and the rumbling vibration stopped as we whipped to the left, back on to the road.

I slid in the opposite direction and hit the passenger-side wall like a forgotten pizza box.

'Hey! It's not a drunk,' Ordonez called back to me. 'The driver's covered in blood. I don't believe it! How do you like this shit? It's your husband!'

He gunned the accelerator even more then. The engine whined, and the van began to wobble dangerously from too much speed.

'White boy thinks he's a badass, huh? Want to play bumper cars?' the dealer sneered into the driver's-side mirror as he floored it.

My stomach dropped when I saw him reach over and click on his shoulder belt. I didn't even have a lap belt to restrain me.

'That's right, you dumb son of a bitch. Catch up, four-eyes! That's it. Now, how do you like . . .'

There was a sudden shriek of metal and rubber as Ordonez slammed on the brakes.

'. . . them apples!' he screamed.

For a moment, the only sound was the whisper of me sliding forward toward the passenger seats.

Then the back of the van blew in with an eardrum-ripping bang.

I did a headstand as the van sprang forward, then a belly flop as it dropped back down with a hard bounce. Through my shock and the gap of the now-bent rear double doors, I saw the smoking front of what had been Paul's Camry. At the very top of the accordioned hood, through the shattered windshield, I could see Paul. He was covered with blood, but blinking at least, as he pawed at the deployed airbag in his lap.

I turned toward Ordonez when I heard a loud metal *clack*. He showed me my own Glock as he opened the door.

'Don't worry, Lauren,' he said. 'Our departure is still right on schedule. Be back in a jiff, honey.'

As he stepped out of the van, one thought pounded through me like a sledgehammer.

He's going to kill Paul! After all this, Paul is going to die!

Chapter Eighty-seven

I screamed then. One of those wordless guttural roars that singed my own ears as I scrambled up with my hands still cuffed behind my back.

Headfirst, reckless, without thinking, I propelled myself toward the open driver's-side door. I missed the open door by a mile, but I did manage to bang my head a nice lick off the steering wheel before I landed upside down in the driver's footwell. Unbelievable.

The idling engine raced as I thrashed against the gas pedal somewhere behind me. I kicked my legs, trying to get some leverage to push myself outside. My foot was stuck between the steering wheel and the gear shift.

I kept kicking, trying to free myself.

Uh-oh.

The gear slid free with my foot, and suddenly the van was rolling, picking up speed!

Based solely on the sudden sound of car horns and the elongated blast from a semi, I guessed that I was rolling into traffic. I'd managed to sit sideways in the footwell by the time Ordonez arrived in the open doorway at a run and jumped in.

'Where do you think you're going, you crazy bitch?' he yelled.

He slapped me across the face before he lifted me up and threw me into the passenger seat, then steered the van back on to the shoulder.

He shut the engine, pulled the emergency brake, and put the keys in his pocket before he stepped outside again.

Then he raised a finger at me and smiled wickedly.

'Okay, let's try this again,' he said. 'You stay ri—'

I never got to hear him finish his sentence. Or his word, for that matter.

The truck that removed him and the van door was a car carrier. Loaded to full capacity with Chevy Tahoes and creaking like a trailer park in a tornado. It must have been doing a good seventy-five or eighty.

One second Mark Ordonez was standing there, and the next he was simply gone. Erased, like in a magic trick.

The best one I'd ever seen.

Chapter Eighty-eight

I sat there, blinking at the van's windshield. The car carrier didn't stop. Didn't even hit its brakes. It was as if the driver hadn't even noticed. A hundred feet or so up the highway, I caught the movement of something sailing end-over-end into the thick roadside brush. Van door or drug dealer, I wasn't sure.

Maybe God had heard my prayers after all. Or heard somebody's prayer for me.

Paul was lying on the ground behind his totaled car. I saw his body as I managed to exit the van. My heart was back in my throat again.

'Paul, I'm here,' I said as I ran and knelt down next to him. I prayed he was okay. CPR was going to be a stretch with my hands cuffed behind my back.

'Lauren,' he said. His teeth started chattering. 'I saw the tail-lights leaving, and I—'

'Don't talk,' I said.

The blood seemed to be coming mostly from the back of Paul's head, where the drug creep had hit him, probably several times. My breath caught as the words *subdural hematoma* flashed from my mental Homicide detective Rolodex. I usually saw it on coroner's reports under cause of death. It seemed like a miracle that Paul was conscious, that either one of us was alive, really.

'Stay still,' I whispered in his ear. 'Don't move.'

Cars whipped past us on the highway as I sat down in the broken glass beside my husband. Blue and red lights started to bubble in the distance. Paul's blood was warm on my legs.

'You saved me, Paul,' I whispered as two state troopers' cars zipped out of the traffic and screeched to a stop in front of us.

Again, I thought, but didn't say. *You saved me again.*

Chapter Eighty-nine

'Milk and sugar okay?' Trooper Harrington said as she came toward me across the UConn Health Center ER waiting room.

Ever since she and the other statie, Trooper Walker, had seen my badge, they had gone above and beyond. Instead of waiting for an ambulance, they laid Paul down in the back of Harrington's cruiser and only asked questions as we headed for the nearest hospital at about 110. Trooper Harrington even loaned me a pair of sneakers from her workout bag in the trunk to put on over my bare and cut-up feet.

'How's your baby and your husband?' she wanted to know.

'The ultrasound showed everything was fine,' I said. 'But Paul has a concussion and needed stitches. They want to keep him overnight for observation. The doctor thinks he's going to be okay, thank God. Thanks to you and your partner.'

'Can't say the same about that Ordonez fella,' the female trooper said with a shake of her head. 'I radioed back to the scene. They found him in the weeds a couple of hundred feet up the road. It was a car carrier that hit him. They said he looks like one of those pennies after you leave it on a railroad track. That's the downside of looking for trouble, isn't it? Sometimes you manage to find a little more than you bargained for.

'Hey, important thing is, you came out on top. You and your husband and your baby. Your family is safe. What else is there?'

I looked into the state trooper's caring face. Her pulled-back blond hair, her scrubbed cheeks, her alert blue-gray eyes brimming with competence. She was maybe one or two years out of the academy. Had I been that earnest once upon a time? I guess I had been. A million years ago, it felt like. And on another planet. I envied her, admired her too.

'So, what's NYC Homicide like?' she said. There was a starstruck glow in her eyes. 'What's it really like? Not like *Law and Order*, I hope.'

'Don't listen to a word she says' came a booming voice from behind us. 'She lies like a rug.'

I turned around toward a smiling face I hadn't seen in a while. In way too long, I decided.

It was my partner, Mike.

'What are you doing here?' I said.

'One of these Connecticut Chip wannabes called Keane, and he called me,' Mike said as he squeezed my hand. 'I came straightaway. The brother came for you, huh? Unbelievable. What a trip. Guess he shoulda stuck to the friendly skies instead of our nation's highways, huh? They pulled him out from underneath a semi or something like that? Nice work, Lauren. That's the best news I've heard all day.'

I nodded my head. Then I finally started crying. I had treated Mike like the enemy, and now here he was, holding my hand, supporting me as always.

'I'm sorry, Mike,' I said. 'I'm . . .'

'Going to buy me a late dinner?' Mike said, linking our elbows as he stood me up. 'Okay, if you insist.'

We found an all-night diner just up the street from the hospital.

'So, what's new, Lauren?' Mike said as we sat. He was back on with the cop humor.

I sipped my coffee in the awkward silence between us. The joe was scalding and bitter. A lot like what I now had to admit.

Mike winked at me.

'C'mon, Lauren. I killed an Ordonez,' he said in a low voice. 'Now you've killed an Ordonez. If you can't talk to me, who else is there?'

I told him everything. Staring into my coffee cup, I recited the whole story. What I knew. When I knew it. Every sordid twist and every tawdry turn.

Mike took a last, loud sip of his Diet Coke and looked out at the passing headlights.

'You know what, Lauren?' he said after a while.

I shook my head.

'Call me screwed up, but even after hearing all that, I'm pretty much glad about what's happened. Maybe they didn't kill Scott, but let's face it, those two Ordonez brethren were an ugly strain of bacteria. And if what brother Mark said about Scott being involved with them was true, then hell, maybe even he had it coming. The Lord,' Mike said, 'He sure do work in mysterious ways.'

Chapter Ninety

I listened to the clattering plates in the diner. Something was sizzling on a grill. On the TV behind the register, a reporter was cackling like an idiot as he was buffeted by the high winds of a Florida storm.

'That's why I'm quitting,' my partner suddenly said. 'My little brother owns a bar in San Juan. He invited me down. I already put my papers in. I'm cashing in all the vacation I've been saving, so today was my last day. I'm out.'

'But . . .'

'But what, Lauren?' Mike said. 'I've put my time in, and you know what? It didn't work out, so screw it. If you make a mistake at a factory and someone gets hurt, what's the worst thing that can happen? You'll lose your job? In our business, you make a mistake, chances are you're losing your job and going to jail. For what? Fifty grand a year? We're not even allowed to go on strike. Please. You know how many dead people I've dealt with? How many grieving mothers? Not worth it. I'm over. What's that song, Lauren? "Even walls fall down."'

I started weeping again then, really crying my eyes out.

'Yeah,' I managed to say. 'And I'm the one holding the sledge-hammer.'

Mike wiped the tears off my cheek with his thumb.

'Bullshit,' he said. 'Me pulling that trigger had nothing to do with you.'

I stared at him.

'Nothing?' I said.

'Well,' he said, pinching his thumb and first finger together. 'Maybe a teensy-weensy bit.'

I punched him in his arm.

'But I forgive you, Lauren,' he said. 'We're partners. But when it comes down to doing the right thing for your family, well, things get hairy quick, don't they? Who am I to judge? No one. Not anymore. That's why I'm out. Though I do regret one thing.'

'What's that?' I said.

'Not being there to see the million-megawatt grin slide off that slick Jeff Buslik's face when you blackmailed him. I always knew you were an ass-kicker, but Christ. You go right for the jugular when you have to.'

'Or lower,' I said, wiping at my red eyes. 'Whatever the situation calls for.'

Mike lifted the ketchup bottle and made the sign of the cross at me with it.

'You are now forgiven for your sins, my child. Go forth unto the earth and sin no more,' he said. 'I mean it, Lauren. You're a good person. Don't ever forget that.'

'I'll try not to, Mike.'

He gave me a kiss on my forehead before he stood.

'And if you ever make your way down to San Juan, you look me up. Ex-partners, even ones involved in super-crazy shit like you, get hooked up with margaritas all night long.'

Chapter Ninety-one

I was coming out of the shower Monday morning of the following week when I found Paul waiting for me. He held my morning coffee in one hand and my fluffy bathrobe in the other. 'What service,' I said, beaming at him. 'I almost can't stand it. Almost.'

'Least I could do, considering what a big day this is,' he said, planting a kiss on my dripping nose.

It was a big day, I thought as I was royally assisted into my robe. I took a sip of the coffee and wiped the steam off the mirror with my sleeve and looked at myself.

My first day back to work.

And the last of my career.

I'd decided to take my partner Mike's lead. I was going to hand in my resignation today, finally get out. It would be a change for me, I knew. It was going to be incredibly hard to get used to not being a cop.

But given what had happened over the past several weeks, I had to admit that it was high time for me to make the move.

Twenty minutes later, my face and badge polished, Paul gave me another kiss at the garage door.

He was dressed for work as well, looking great, handsome as ever. His concussion, like the doctors had thought, had only been minor, thank God. Except for twenty or so stitches at the back of his head, he was as good as new.

He too was wrapping things up at work. It was all arranged now. We'd gotten the paperwork from the relocation company on Friday. Both closings were set. Paul's new Connecticut job and our new Connecticut life would start in six weeks.

If we could get through the next eight hours.

Not exactly a sure thing, considering our recent history. I crossed my fingers as I raised my travel mug to his.

'The family that quits the rat race together . . .' I said.

'Stays together,' Paul said as the clink of stainless steel echoed off the walls of the garage.

Chapter Ninety-two

I caught Lieutenant Keane in his office when I came into the squad room. He only looked up from his *Post* sudoku puzzle after I closed his door.

Then his sharp blue eyes scanned my face. Suddenly he slapped his paper and pen on to his desk.

'Please,' he said. 'Not you too. Don't tell me you're leaving. You can't. How does that make sense, Lauren? We lose one cop, and now two more are gone?'

'It's not like that, LT. You're reading this wrong.'

'Please. Do I look stupid? If it's IAB you're worried about, I have hooks and—'

'I'm pregnant, Pete,' I said.

Keane stared at me as if I'd shot a round into the ceiling. He rubbed at his eyes with his fingertips. Finally, reluctantly, he smiled. Then he stood and walked around his desk and gave me a fatherly hug. The first, I believe, he'd ever given me. Probably the last, too.

'Well, young lady, even though I don't remember giving you permission to get pregnant, congratulations to you and Paul. I'm happy for you both.'

'I appreciate it, bossman.'

'You had some trouble too, if I remember. Ann and I did too

– before the twins. That's just terrific for you guys. You have to be ecstatic. I'm sickened by the fact you're completely screwing me by leaving, but I'll get used to it, I suppose. I'm sure as hell going to miss you. I guess going out and tying one on is out of the question. How can we celebrate? How about some break-fast?'

My boss ordered in from the precinct's local bodega, and we sat for half the morning, telling old stories as we ate scrambled egg quesadillas and drank coffee.

'Hey, if I'd known it was going to be this much fun,' I said, wiping hot sauce off my cheek, 'I would have retired years ago.'

Keane's desk phone rang as we were finishing our coffee.

'Yeah?' he called into it.

'That's weird. That's very strange. Okay, send her up, I guess.'

'Send up who?' I asked, an edge creeping into my voice.

'The witness in Scott's case. What's her name? The old school-marm?'

My heart and stomach did a simultaneous stutter step.

Amelia Phelps!

What now?

'What does she want?' I asked.

Keane pointed his sharp chin out at the rail of the squad room stairs, where Amelia Phelps was standing.

'You can start your two weeks' notice by finding out. Go talk to her.'

I got right up and walked out to see what was up.

'Yes, Mrs – I mean, Ms Phelps,' I said, leading her to my desk. 'What can I do for you today?'

'I was expecting to get a call to come in and look at a lineup,' she said, removing her white gloves as she sat. 'But no one ever got in touch, so I thought I'd stop by and ask if I can be of any assistance.'

I let out a long breath of relief. Mike must have forgotten to let her know we wouldn't need her after all.

'I'm sorry, Ms Phelps, I should have called you. It turns out we apprehended the suspect, so we no longer need your help. It was so good of you to come in, though. Can I give you a ride somewhere? Back to your house maybe? It wouldn't be any trouble.'

I usually wasn't in the business of chauffeuring witnesses, but Ms Phelps was elderly. And besides, she was the last conceivable wrinkle in the whole ordeal. The sooner I got her out of there, the better.

'Oh, okay,' she said. 'That would be very nice, Detective. I've never actually ridden in a police car before. Thank you.'

'Believe me,' I said, steering her toward the exit. 'It's no problem at all.'

Chapter Ninety-three

The rest of the day I spent on the phone with personnel. *On hold* with personnel was more like it as I attempted to hash out the bureaucratic details of my resignation.

Periodically, my fellow squaddies came by to register their surprise and good wishes. They even insisted I head out with them around four to The Sportsmen, the precinct's local gin mill, for a farewell drink.

Though my bladder came dangerously close to bursting point at the bar – with Diet Cokes, of course – I was deeply touched by my co-workers' concern and respect.

They even gave me one of those corny, oversize greeting cards with what had to be the entire precinct's signatures.

See ya, it said on the front.

And on the inside, *Wouldn't wanna be ya.*

Who knew Hallmark had a NYC Cop Attitude section?

'Oh, guys,' I said with a sniffle. 'I'm going to miss you too. And I wouldn't want to *be ya* either.'

It was around seven when I finally begged out of there and headed for home.

That's funny, I thought, as I pulled into my driveway. I didn't see Paul's car. He usually called to let me know when he had to work late.

I was opening the call file on my cell to ring him, when I noticed something kind of strange in the den window over the garage.

There was a dark gap in the slats of the blinds. As I scrolled down for Paul's cell number, I tried to remember the last time I'd opened them.

I looked back up, slowly, very deliberately, then shut my cell phone with a click.

The gap in the blinds had closed.

Wait a second, I thought. *Hold on.*

My mind raced as I thought of the possibilities. Could this be more friends of the Ordonezes? Maybe there was another brother I didn't know about?

Or maybe you're just tired and paranoid, I thought. Maybe one too many Diet Cokes at The Sportsmen.

I pulled out my Glock and put it in the belt of my skirt at the back.

Most definitely a little skittish, I thought. But better paranoid than sorry.

Chapter Ninety-four

I took out my keys as I came up the stairs, acting as naturally as I could. When I was out of sight of the den window, I drew my gun and ran around to the back of my house.

I glanced at the windows. Everything seemed intact. No sign of a break-in. No trouble so far.

There was a small gap in the curtains at the back door. I peered through it, watching the front-to-back hallway for a while. No movement. Nothing.

After a few minutes, I began to feel silly. There was nobody there but me.

Then, at the end near the door, something suddenly crossed through the dark hall. A large shadow moving quickly. I was sure of it.

Shit! I thought as my pulse pounded. Christ! I could feel my heartbeat in the fillings of my teeth.

That's when I thought of Paul. Maybe he actually was home. And there was somebody in there with him. Running around in the dark. Who? For what possible reason?

I had to go inside, I decided with a deep breath.

I slipped off my shoes and, with painstaking quiet, unlocked the back door and turned the knob, as slowly as I could.

'*Shh,*' I heard somebody say. Not me.

I was lifting my Glock toward the sound, ready to squeeze off a shot, when the lights went on.

'SURPRISE!' said a couple of dozen voices in unison.

I'll say! Jesus God, it was my friends and family. The female ones, at least. By some miracle, I didn't fire a round. Thank goodness for safe-action pistols.

I gaped at the Mylar balloons, the green-and-yellow-wrapped presents, the three-wheel yuppie jogging stroller parked in the corner.

It wasn't a home invasion after all. Not bad news or tragedy.

It was my baby shower!

And judging by the number of hands that shot up over open-mouthed, blood-drained faces, I guessed it had been a real surprise all around.

I lowered my sights from between my elderly Aunt Lucy's eyes. She started breathing again.

'Look, Mommy,' my sister Michele's four-year-old daughter said in the dead silence. 'Auntie Lauren has a gun.'

'It's all right, ladies,' Paul said, smiling as he hurried forward and helped me to reholster my weapon. He gave me a hug to help me recover.

'Why did you plan the shower for now? I'm only eleven weeks,' I whispered as he kissed me on the cheek.

'I wanted to make sure you got a shower before the move,' Paul said, turning back toward the crowd. 'Now, smile. Big smile. Enjoy your party.

'It's all right,' he repeated. 'Just another day in the life of a hero cop. Thank God we have a fresh supply of diapers, huh? Who needs a drink?'

Chapter Ninety-five

T he shower was a big success – happy times for all, but especially for me. I had such good friends, and even my relatives
were mostly nice. Life was finally starting to make some sense
again. And then—

'Hey, stranger!' Bonnie Clesnik said, dropping her menu and
almost knocking the table over as she hugged me in the middle
of the Mott Street Dragon Flower the Sunday after the baby
shower.

I looked around at the overly bright restaurant. There were
cloudy-looking fish tanks everywhere. When my old CSU sergeant
friend Bonnie called me to come out with her, I was thinking pub
grub, home fries, a couple of Virgin Marys maybe.

I blinked as I picked up the menu and saw the picture of a
turtle and a frog. Wow. Sunday brunch in Chinatown. I guess
Bonnie had never had morning sickness herself.

'I can't believe I missed your retirement party and your shower,'
Bonnie said as we sat. 'Someone on third shift called in sick, and
wouldn't you know it? I got the call.'

'Save the regrets, Bonnie,' I said, smiling. 'It's me here. This is
great. Perfect.' As long as I can keep the Chinese food down.

'So,' Bonnie said midway through the dim sum. 'All of a sudden, it's so many changes for you. I would have thought they'd have to pry you off The Job with a hammer and a crowbar. I'm so happy for you and Paul, of course, but . . . I don't know. I've seen how you work cases, Lauren. The glow in your eyes. How fearless you can be. I'm not the only woman cop you've inspired either, by the way. I guess it's hard for me to see you turn it all down and walk away. Somehow I can't see you as a soccer mom.'

Gee, Bonnie. Thanks for the vote of confidence, I thought. Wasn't this supposed to be a celebration? Let the good times flow?

Suddenly, Bonnie laid down her chopsticks.

'Before I forget,' she said, 'I have a gift.'

She removed a large manila envelope from her bag and handed it to me. I opened the flap.

'Just what I've always wanted,' I said, looking at the pages and then staring at my friend quizzically. 'A computer printout.'

What was going on now?

'I received that on Friday from the FBI lab,' Bonnie said. She dabbed at her mouth with her napkin and looked into my eyes with kind concern. 'It's the results from the DNA sample I found on the tarp Scott Thayer was found wrapped in.'

The world whited out for a second as a sudden heat flash sizzled through me.

Our goddamned Neat Sheet! I actually remembered the picnic where Paul had provided his DNA sample!

It was our first anniversary. Paul had brought me and two bottles of champagne up to the exquisitely beautiful Rockwood Hall Park in North Tarrytown. Had it ever gotten better for us? I doubted it. Late summer. Champagne and crickets, and just the two of us. It was the first time we'd actually tried to get pregnant.

I glanced at the pages, then back at my friend.

'What are you talking about?' I asked Bonnie. 'I thought that you said all you could find was Scott's blood.'

'After I scraped it off, I noticed that there was another, older stain. It turns out it was dried semen. Just enough to get a DNA signature.'

I squinted at the pages. What would it take for Scott's case to stay closed? I wondered. Holy water? Pounding a stake through its heart? Shooting it with a silver bullet?

And what the hell was I supposed to say now? Bonnie seemed to be waiting for something from me.

'Why didn't you tell me about this before?' I finally got up the courage to ask.

'I tried to,' Bonnie said. 'But it was the morning of the Ordonez shooting, and I couldn't reach you. When I called your lieutenant the next day, he told me to shit-can it. They'd found Scott's gun on Victor Ordonez, and the case was a slam-dunk.'

'So what's the problem?' I said.

Bonnie let out a sigh.

'What can I tell you, kid? The DNA isn't from Ordonez. And yeah, I'm sure.'

I ran through the implications at the speed of light. They had Paul's DNA! That would be devastating for him, for both of us. And baby makes three.

'Whose is it?' I said carefully.

'We don't know,' Bonnie answered.

Thank God for small mercies, I thought.

But unfortunately Bonnie wasn't done.

'But we did get a cold hit from another crime scene,' she said. 'How about that?'

What?! How about I shoot myself here in the Dragon Flower?

A vague and sickening dread hit the center of my chest like a punch.

'Run that by me again,' I said to Bonnie.

'The Feds' CODIS database collects DNA samples from crime scenes across the country in order to ID perpetrators. It turns out the same DNA from the semen on the blanket in your case was found at another crime scene – an armed robbery in Washington, DC. Happened nearly five years ago. The case was never closed.'

The dread that had been operating in my stomach suddenly shifted its strategy for attack and caught me in a hammerlock around the throat. I was having trouble thinking, even sitting in an upright position.

No. It couldn't be. What Bonnie was saying meant that . . .

Paul had been involved in another crime? An armed robbery?

Chapter Ninety-six

The waiter came and Bonnie paid. Then she reached across the table and patted my shaking hands.

'I didn't mean to drop all of this on you at once, Lauren,' she said. 'I was as shocked as you are.'

Want to bet? I thought, dropping my eyes to the table.

'An armed robbery in DC?' I whispered through the cotton that had suddenly materialized in my mouth. 'You're sure about it, Bonnie?'

'The brief abstract they sent with the positive match said the DNA came from a blood sample found at an armed robbery in a DC hotel. But the case wasn't solved, and it's still open. The match means that we have anonymous secretions at two different crime scenes. Semen on the blanket used to cover Thayer. And blood in some DC hotel room.'

What did that mean? Obviously, they still didn't know it was Paul's. As if that mattered, I thought, dropping my pulverized head into my hands. As if anything did at this point.

Bonnie kept talking but I barely heard what she was saying. All I could do was blink and nod. The impossible had just happened. For the first time in a while, I had actually managed to stop caring about Scott's case. I had a new distraction.

Almost five years ago Paul had committed some kind of armed robbery in a hotel room? My brain labored over that thought, then promptly went on strike.

Because that was impossible.

But DNA doesn't lie.

When I looked up, I found Bonnie staring at me, waiting for some kind of comment.

'So what does this mean?' I said, as if I didn't know the answer. 'Victor Ordonez didn't kill Scott Thayer?'

Bonnie looked out the window on to crowded Mott Street. There was pain in her eyes.

'I don't know. How could I, Lauren? Maybe he just borrowed the blanket off a friend, but it definitely throws some doubt out there, doesn't it?' she said. 'The kind of doubt a defense lawyer would have a field day with. Not to mention the press jackals.'

I looked at the neon Chinese characters in the restaurant window. A black eel in the aquarium beside our booth batted his head against the glass as if trying to get my attention and say something. *Hey, Lauren. Why don't you just run screaming out of the restaurant? Don't stop till you get to Bellevue.*

Bonnie straightened the papers against the tabletop, pushed them back into the envelope, and stuffed the whole thing down into my bag.

'But I decided it's the kind of doubt this city, this department, Scott's wife, and most especially you, Lauren, don't need thrown out there.'

She gestured toward my handbag.

'That's why I'm giving it to you, honey. This case was screwed for everyone involved from the word go. This is my retirement present to you. The DC detective's name and contact info are somewhere in those sheets, if you ever want to pursue it on your own. Or you can chuck it off the Brooklyn Bridge. Your choice.'

Bonnie planted a big kiss on my forehead as she stood up at our table.

'One thing I've learned as a cop is that you do what you can. It's not our fault that sometimes that's not enough. Lauren, you're my friend, and I love you, and it's up to you. See you around.'

Chapter Ninety-seven

It was a few hours later, and dark, when I found myself standing in Battery Park at the southern tip of Manhattan.

Manhattan, my father used to say before he'd start his thrice-weekly walks from this very park. *The greatest treadmill in the world.*

His post-retirement exercise routine consisted of riding the subway here to the last stop, walking over to Broadway, and seeing how many of Manhattan's thirteen concrete miles he could cover before he got tired and hopped on an uptown subway headed back home. All through law school, I'd go with him if I had the chance. Listen to him talk about the crimes and arrests that had occurred at the countless intersections. It was on one of those walks with Dad that I decided I wanted to be a cop rather than a lawyer. Wanted to be just like my father.

And it was right here, at the beginning of one of those walks, all alone, that he died of a heart attack. As if he'd have it no other way than to pass on the streets of the city he'd served and loved.

I rested the FBI report against the rusted railing before me as I listened to the dark waves slap against the concrete pier.

Just when I'd completed the toughest puzzle ever, Dad, I thought.

I'd been handed an extra piece.

Story of my life recently.

'What do I do, Pop?' I whispered as tears fell down my cheeks. 'I don't know what to do.'

There were exactly two options, I knew.

I could toss away Bonnie's gift, like I had the rest of the evidence, and head to my new life in Connecticut, a blissful soccer-mom-to-be.

Or I could slap myself out of my denial and figure out what the hell was going on with my life, and with my mysterious husband.

I held the envelope over the railing.

This was an easy one, right?

All I had to do was release my fingers and it would be over.

I would go to the train and head north, where safety, my husband, and my new life waited.

A gust of wind picked up off the water, flapping the envelope in my hand.

Let it go, I thought. Let it go, let it go.

But finally I dug my nails into the envelope and clutched it to my chest.

I couldn't. I needed to get to the bottom of this, no matter how hard, how ugly, it got. Even after everything I had pulled, all the craziness, all the hurting my friends and covering things up, I guess there was still some scrap of detective left in me. Maybe more than a scrap.

I closed my eyes tightly. Somewhere in the darkness of the park behind me, I sensed an old man stretching his legs, limbering up for a walk. As I turned around quickly to find a taxi, out of the corner of my eye I felt a figure nodding in my direction, a smile on his face.

Chapter Ninety-eight

It was a little after eight the next morning when the barista at the Starbucks across from Paul's Pearl Street office building raised an eyebrow at me in surprise.

Jeez, I thought. You'd think she'd never seen a disheveled, emotionally demolished woman ask for the entire top shelf of the pastry case before.

After last night's Battery Park epiphany, I'd called Paul and told him that Bonnie wanted me to stay over in the city for old times' sake. Then I'd wandered up Broadway, like the homeless person I now was, until about midnight.

I'd made it all the way to The Midtown, just south of the Ed Sullivan Theater, when my legs quit on me.

I had just enough strength to toss the questionable orange-speckled bedspread into the corner of my three-hundred-dollar-a-night closet before I passed out. Pretty pricey, but Paul could afford it.

I woke up at 7 a.m., left the hotel without showering, and caught a taxi on Seventh Avenue, heading downtown to the financial district.

For the first time in a month, I had a game plan. I knew exactly what I had to do.

Interrogate Paul.

I didn't care what it took. I'd be both good cop and bad cop. I was tempted to bring the hotel phone book along in case I had to beat the truth out of him. One thing was certain. Paul was going to tell me what the hell was going on if it was the last thing he ever did.

And based on the way I was feeling as I stood in the Starbucks across from his office, that was a distinct possibility.

'Anything else?' the barista asked, pushing my five-figure-calorie breakfast across the counter.

'You don't have anything else,' I told her.

In an oversize purple velvet wing chair positioned by the window, I read the FBI report, cover to cover.

I stared at the autoradiographs – the DNA vertical barcodes – for both crime scenes until my vision blurred.

There was no mistake, no denying what the pages said. I didn't have to know what *variable number tandem repeat* meant or what the heck an *STR locus* was to see that the two samples were one and the same.

I put the report down, and with one eye on the revolving doors of Paul's black-glass office building across the narrow street, I commenced a world-record round of compulsive eating. Hey, alcohol and nicotine were out. What's a very pissed-off, pregnant cop supposed to do?

I was licking chocolate icing off my fingers fifteen minutes later when, through the scrum of business suits and power ties, I spotted the sandy head of a man Paul's height turning into the office building. Good-looking guy, no denying it. That was one constant about my husband. Maybe the only one.

I knocked back the last of an espresso brownie, slowly brushed myself off, and grabbed the latte-stained FBI report.

Come out with your hands up, Paul, I thought as I crossed the still-shadowy canyon of Pearl Street. Your pissed-off, pregnant wife has a gun in her handbag.

But as I stood in line behind a FedEx guy at the security desk, I noticed something odd.

Paul was in the open door of one of the elevators.

Here we go again, I thought.

Unlike the rest of the invading, pin-striped financial army, he was making his way out, like a salmon swimming upstream, a lone salmon.

Whatever, I thought, taking a quick step toward him through the crowd. This saves me an elevator trip.

But as I got closer, I noticed the carry-on strapped across his chest. And the shopping bag in his hand.

The blue Tiffany shopping bag.

I stopped dead-still, and stayed silent as I watched him head toward the doorway.

Chapter Ninety-nine

*C*arry-on? Tiffany bag? Where was Paul going? What the hell was happening now? Did I really want to know?

Yes! I needed to find out, I decided, as I watched him flag a taxi.

His cab was pulling out when I whistled and caught the next one pulling in.

'At the risk of sounding clichéd,' I told the orange-turbaned driver, 'follow that cab.'

So we did. Up to Midtown Manhattan. Then through the Midtown Tunnel on to the Long Island Expressway.

When our cabs reached the Brooklyn-Queens Expressway, I called Paul's cell.

'Hey, Paul. What's up?' I said when he answered after a couple of ring-a-dings.

'Lauren,' Paul said. 'How was your sleepover?' I could actually see him through the rear window of the taxi in front of me, holding his cell to his ear.

'Terrific,' I said. 'Listen, Paul. I'm bored out of my mind. I was thinking of heading down to see you for lunch today. What do you say? That be okay?'

Here it is, Paul. Your moment of truth.

'Can't, babe,' Paul said. 'You know Mondays are impossible. We got six earnings reports coming in that have to be crunched and recrunched. I can see my boss from my desk right now. He's knocking back beta-blockers with his venti. If I get out of here by eight tonight, I'll be lucky. I'm sorry. I'll make it up to you, promise. How are you feeling?'

The green sign we were speeding under said 'LaGuardia Airport.' I had to hold my hand over the mouthpiece on my cell in order to muffle a sob.

'Just fine, Paul,' I said after a second. 'Don't worry about me. See you tonight.' *If not sooner, babe!*

At the airport, I had to flash my badge and NYPD ID in order to get past the security checkpoint without a ticket. Then I stayed well back in the torrent of people as I followed Paul down the departures concourse, past the regiments of newsstands and gift shops and open bars.

He stopped suddenly, about a hundred feet ahead of me, and sat down at Gate 32.

Keeping my distance by a bank of pay phones, I felt like an ulcer exploded open in my stomach when I saw his destination.

Washington, DC.

Chapter One Hundred

I t cost me $175 to snag a last-minute seat on Paul's flight. What was I saying? It cost Paul $175. *Excellent.*

Watching from a restaurant across the departure concourse, I literally flinched as Paul was checking in for the business-class boarding call.

That was because the flight attendant at the counter did something more than a little odd after he handed Paul his ticket stub.

He punched Paul's fist playfully – as if they were old pals! What was that all about?

If there was a good thing to say about my second-to-last back-row seat in coach, it was that there was no way for Paul and me to bump into each other. Oh, and it had a handy barf bag. One that I made use of promptly after take-off.

Pregnancy and motion sickness and watching your world going up in apocalyptic flames – really bad combination.

'Sorry,' I said to my thoroughly disturbed female executive neighbor, who was on the phone. 'Baby on the way. Morning has broken.'

The really tricky part came when we landed in Washington. Paul, along with the rest of the corporate-class dweebs, got off first. So I really had to hightail it out to the arrival gate in order to see which way he'd gone.

But by the time I'd made it to the taxi line on the street, there was no sign of him.

Damn it, damn it, damn it! What a waste this whole trip down here had been.

I was doubling back, heading up the escalator, when I saw him coming out of the men's room. He'd changed into jeans and a nice blue sweater – and he wasn't wearing his glasses anymore.

What kept me from screaming his name right then and there, I don't know. His ass was so busted it was unreal.

Instead, I just double-timed it back down the stairs and continued to trail my deceitful husband.

I needed to know firsthand just how deep he'd sunk the blade into my back.

Paul went directly past the taxi line through the sliding glass doors into the street. The doors were closing when I saw him do something that made me stop in my tracks and just stare.

He opened the passenger door of a shiny black Range Rover that was idling at the curb.

I decided to run then.

By the time I'd made it ten feet outside, the sleek luxury SUV was already moving, tires shrieking as it cut off a minibus and shot into the left lane.

My eyes strained to get the license plate number as I ran across the exhaust-stained pavement after it.

It was a DC plate starting with 99.

I gave up on the rest of the number and tried to get a quick look at the driver. I wanted to see who, or more specifically what gender, the person was who had just picked up my husband.

But the windows were tinted. I discovered that little fact about the same moment that I tripped over a golf bag and gave the hallowed ground of our nation's capital an enthusiastic, chest-bumping high-five.

Chapter One Hundred and One

Not exactly sure where to start looking for Paul, I decided to pay Roger Zampella, the contact detective listed in the FBI report, a visit.

I'd never met Roger face-to-face, of course. He turned out to be a large, well-dressed African-American with a smile brighter than the polished buckles of his polka-dot suspenders.

When I called him from the airport, he'd immediately invited me over to his squad room at the Metro DC Second District Station on Idaho Avenue. I arrived to catch him just beginning an early lunch at his desk.

'You don't mind if I eat while we talk, do you, Detective?' he said, flipping his silk pink-and-green repp tie over his shoulder. He tucked a napkin into the white collar of his two-tone baby-blue banker's shirt before upending a brown lunch bag on to his desk with a flourish.

A small apple slid out, along with a Quaker oatmeal bar about the size of a used bar of soap.

He cleared his throat.

'My wife,' he explained as he tore open the bar's wrapper with his teeth, 'just saw the results of my latest cholesterol test. I got an F-minus. You said on the phone you wanted to talk to me about a robbery? I should have told you, I'm in Homicide now.'

'It's actually from nearly five years ago,' I said. 'I was wondering if you could recall anything about it. The case number was three-seven-three-four-five. An armed robbery at the Sheraton Crystal City Hotel in Arlington, Virginia, across the river from the capital. The perpetrator—'

'Left some blood,' Detective Zampella said without any hesitation. 'The ticket-broker thing. I remember it.'

'You have a good memory,' I said.

'You never forget the open ones, unfortunately,' he said.

'You said something about a ticket broker?'

Zampella sniffed at the oatmeal bar before he took a dainty squirrel nibble.

'The Sheraton, this is the one out near Reagan National Airport, was hosting the annual NCAA football coaches' convention,' he said as he chewed. 'All the big schools' coaches and assistant coaches receive Final Four tickets every year for free. These ticket brokers – glorified ticket scalpers, if you want my opinion – just set up shop in the hotel and buy them up. Pay out cash right there and then. Illegal, of course, but we're talking about college recruiters. They've been known to bend a few rules.'

'How much cash are we talking about here, Roger?'

'A lot,' Zampella said. 'Some of the games go for a thousand bucks a ticket.'

'And there was a robbery?'

Zampella went to take another little bite, decided to hell with it, and dropped the whole thing into his mouth. He chewed twice, swallowed, then cleared his throat.

'One of these brokers apparently came down a couple of nights before the convention,' he said. 'And somebody must have gotten wind of who he was, and they robbed him of his suitcase of cash.'

'Get a description?' I said. 'Anything at all?'

Zampella shook his head.

'Guy wore a ski mask.'

A ski mask? Wow, Paul was really original. Not to mention completely insane.

'Where'd the blood come from? Anybody figure that out?'

'When the broker was handing over the case, he had second thoughts and hit the thief in the chin with it. Guy was a bleeder, I guess. Ruined the carpet.'

'What did the thief do then?'

'He took out a gun, threatened to blow the broker away. That's when he gave the case up.'

'How much did the thief get?'

'Half a million, maybe more. The victim said it was only seven thousand, but that's because he didn't want to get in trouble with the IRS, or maybe the Mob. This guy was a major ticket broker.'

'Suspects?' I said.

'There was no hit on the blood. We interviewed several guests on the broker's floor. There were, like, two thousand people at the conference that night. We weren't going to set the world on fire for some slick, probably Mobbed-up asshole ticket broker who was tripping over himself to lie to us. We went by the book and, you know how it is, moved on to the next thing, forgot all about it. Until now, that is. What are you doing? Gathering new material for a revival of *Unsolved Mysteries*?'

'It's actually personal,' I told the detective. 'A friend of mine, a jeweler, was pistol-whipped and robbed in a Midtown Manhattan hotel last month. I remembered seeing the abstract on your case when I looked into it. You wouldn't happen to have a copy of the hotel register, would you?'

'I did put one in the file,' Zampella said, checking his watch. 'But it's been – what? Five years? God knows where they buried it.'

'I know I'm being a pain in the neck,' I said. 'But do you think you could make a couple of calls and track it down for me? After I take you out for lunch, of course. DC has a Morton's, doesn't it?'

Zampella glanced at his scrawny apple. Then he reached for his pin-striped suit jacket on the back of his chair.

'As a matter of fact,' he said, standing up, 'there's one right here in Arlington.'

Chapter One Hundred and Two

Two hours and two filet mignons with home fries later, we were back in Zampella's office, and I was going over the very hotel register I needed to see so urgently.

Zampella thought *he* had heart trouble? When I glanced at the top of the second page, I could have used a defibrillator *and* a shot of epinephrine.

There it was in black and white – *Paul Stillwell.*

Something inside me swayed dangerously. Even after all the evidence, I was hoping for some eleventh-hour reprieve. Yet here was the opposite. More and more proof of Paul's – what? Lunacy? Secret life?

I couldn't believe it. Paul had actually robbed a sports ticket broker of half a million dollars?

And I'd thought finding out secret stuff about Scott Thayer was devastating. What the hell was wrong with men? Were they all legally insane?

No, I answered myself. Not all of them. Just the ones who had the misfortune to make my acquaintance. Or the other way around.

I thought about the Range Rover and the Tiffany bag and

the fact that Paul didn't wear glasses down here in DC.

I turned to Zampella, half snoozing behind his desk. He'd had a martini with his steak.

'You think you could do me just one more favor, Roger? Just one, and I'm gone.'

'Shoot,' he said.

'I'm looking for an owner's list of 2007 Range Rovers. DC plates starting with ninety-nine.'

'More *Unsolved Mysteries* material, huh? All right, you got it. But fraternal order of police cooperation aside, this has to be the last one. My lieutenant is due back from a department conference any second. There's a bookstore right down the block. Why don't you catch up on some reading, and I'll see you in about an hour.'

It was more like half an hour. I was sitting in front of the magazine rack, paging through a *Vanity Fair,* when Zampella tapped me on the shoulder.

'I think you dropped something, miss,' he said, handing me an envelope with a wink before heading off toward the exit.

I ripped the sheet of paper out of the envelope. The list was twenty-one vehicles long. I traced my finger down the owner's column, looking for Stillwell.

No dice. I did it again more slowly. Again nothing.

I rubbed my overcaffeinated tired eyes. What the hell? It was worth a shot.

I went into the bookstore's café, sat down, and pulled out the hotel guest list. One by one, I cross-referenced each Range Rover owner with the hotel list. It was maybe fifteen minutes later, pins and needles tingling my butt, when I found a match.

Veronica Boyd. 221 Riggs Place.

Veronica? I thought, seething. I knew it! A woman! Paul, you goddamned bastard!

I jumped out of my seat and bolted for the front door. I needed to rent a car. And maybe do some surveillance work.

It was time to find out exactly what – oh, and most especially *who* – Paul had done.

Chapter One Hundred
and Three

The house was a quaint attached brick residence on a low-key but definitely upscale street in a neighborhood north of Dupont Circle. The rainbow flags outside the coffee bars and the restaurants housed in its old stately buildings reminded me a lot of Greenwich Village, the more yuppified parts, anyway.

From my rented Ford Taurus parked at the corner, I kept my eyes locked on the gleaming black door of 221 Riggs Place.

A quick scan of the block didn't reveal any black Range Rovers among the several other brands of luxury vehicles parked along both sides of the narrow, tree-lined street.

Well, what do you know? I thought, squinting at the shutter-lined upper windows of the house. In his secret life Paul seemed to be doing darn well for himself.

But was it his house? I truly didn't want it to be. If I ever wanted to be completely wrong about something, it was this.

Let there be some explanation, Paul. Something I can stomach.

An hour later, I was about to take a spin for a restroom break when the front door finally opened. None other than Paul came down the brick stoop of the town house, carrying the blue Tiffany bag.

He pressed the key fob in his hand, and the headlights of a hunter-green convertible Jaguar on the far corner glowed with a double *bloop*.

That really wasn't fair, I thought, sublimating the urge to plow the rented car broadside into the Jaguar. Why couldn't we have the Jag in our dimension?

Next up, I tailed Paul through the afternoon traffic. We made a turn on to 14th Street and passed a bunch of lettered side streets, S Street, R. I followed him left on to Q Street, then right on to 13th Street and around the rotary to O Street. I watched as he pulled into the parking lot of an ivy-covered brick building.

The Chamblis School, said a brass sign on its wall. This couldn't be good. Not a chance in hell that this was the happy ending I was looking for.

I parked at a hydrant, feeling like I was in a trance as I watched Paul get out of the Jag, carrying the Tiffany bag.

Veronica Boyd was a teacher? I could just about picture her. Preppy and little and blonde. Not to mention young. And very attractive, of course.

Was that what this was all about? I thought, starting to fume in the car. Out with the old, in with the new?

I watched Paul return to the Jag three minutes later.

What in the world?

She was young, all right.

A three- or four-year-old girl wearing a plaid jumper threw her arms around Paul's neck. He closed his eyes as he hugged her and then opened the bag. The little girl removed a white teddy bear wearing a silver necklace and kissed it.

Paul lifted her up under her arms and carefully put her and the teddy bear into the car.

I was still sitting, immobilized, when Paul maneuvered the purring Jag around the wagons, SUVs, and Hummers of the other parents picking up their kids. When he stopped at the corner, I got a good look at the girl through the back window.

My lungs quit. No inhaling. No exhaling.

I recognized that pin-straight nose, those blue eyes, that sandy hair. The girl was as beautiful as Paul was handsome. She'd gotten all of his looks.

I couldn't believe it, absolutely couldn't. The pain was unreal, impossible to imagine without actually experiencing it, open-heart surgery without anesthesia.

Things were a thousand times worse than I'd ever thought they could be. Paul had pulled off the cruelest trick possible.

A baby, I thought.

Paul had had a baby.

Without me.

Chapter One Hundred
and Four

I arrived back at 221 Riggs Place just in time to see Paul coming back out of the house with his little girl and a Dora the Explorer bike complete with training wheels. I nodded ironically as he popped the smiling child on to it and headed the bicycle south down the sidewalk.

Off to the playground, no doubt. I always knew Paul would make an excellent father.

When they were out of sight, I emerged from the Taurus and headed for the stoop. Just one more thing to do here, I thought as I climbed the stairs mechanically and rang the doorbell. One final detail to take care of.

I just needed to core out the very last remnants of my heart.

'Yes?' said the woman who opened the door.

She was blonde, all right, but not preppy. And not little. At least not her chest. I guessed she was about my age, which, honestly, didn't help one bit. I scrutinized her heavy-handed makeup, the way her tight black skirt cut into her tummy. She looked like she'd recently put on weight.

An attractive woman desperately battling the onslaught of her late thirties. Welcome to the club.

I stared into her dark brown eyes under the razor streaks of blond, an off-putting clash of light and dark. When I smelled her perfume, something cold drew across my stomach. Like a razor.

'Veronica?' I finally spoke.

'Yes,' she said again. I noticed she had an accent, Texan maybe, definitely southern.

I took out my badge.

'I'm Detective Stillwell,' I said. 'May I please have a word with you?'

'What's this about?' she said tensely, not budging from the doorway. I couldn't tell if she knew me or just didn't like badges.

I took out the DMV printout I'd gotten from Zampella.

'Do you have a 2007 black Range Rover?' I asked the blonde woman. Paul's other wife?

'Yes,' she said. 'What about it?'

'I'm investigating a hit-and-run accident. May I come in? It will only take a moment.'

'Why does a New York City detective want to investigate a hit-and-run accident in Washington, DC?' she asked, keeping herself wedged in the doorway.

I already had an answer for that. 'I'm sorry. I should have explained. My mother came down three days ago with her church group. She was the victim. If there's some sort of problem, I could always just go ahead and have your vehicle impounded.'

'Come in,' she said, stepping to the side. 'This has to be some kind of mistake.'

There was an off-white pub mirror and a cute espresso-stained mail desk in the front foyer. The design was contemporary, moderately tasteful. The rooms were sunny and cozy.

She led me into the kitchen, where she'd opted for retro appliances. A pink mixer sat on the butcher-block island next to a bag of flour. She was cooking dinner for Paul? Sweet girl.

'My daughter Caroline's fourth birthday is today, and I have to make a Dora the Explorer cake or the world will end,' Veronica said, staring into my eyes.

The world *has* ended, I felt like saying as I looked away.

'Coffee?' she asked.

'That would be fine,' I said. 'Thank you.'

She opened and closed a cupboard over the sink. I stood there light-headed, fighting to stay on my feet. What the heck was I doing here? What was I trying to get out of this?

Down the hallway, I spotted a vanity wall, photographs on floating shelves.

'May I use your bathroom?' I asked.

'Down the hall to your right.'

The walls of the hall seemed to collapse in on me as I saw Paul in one of the photos. He was on a sunny beach with Veronica and the baby, who was maybe one at the time. Surf spraying, the sand like powdered sugar. The next shot – *to my heart* – was of the two of them, Mommy and Daddy, their cheeks together in midlaugh, red-eyed with city lights twinkling behind them.

The third photograph hit me like a serrated blade between my eyes. A half-naked Veronica in an open nightgown, Paul resting his chin on her shoulder as he cupped her ripe, pregnant belly in his hands.

By the time I got to the fourth, and final, photo, a thousand-megaton blast in my skull had mushroomed. *Paul, you bastard.*

Veronica's breath was suddenly at my back.

'You're not here to ask about some car accident,' she announced.

I stared at their wedding photo for another moment, dry-eyed. It had been taken on the same beach as the first photograph. A minister was there. White flowers in Veronica's blonde hair. Paul in an open-throated white silk shirt. Smiling. Beaming, actually.

She wisely jumped out of my way as I stumbled toward the front door.

Chapter One Hundred and Five

It had all been for nothing! Not just everything that had happened in the past month – my entire marriage.

That thought hummed like high-voltage electricity through my head as I drifted in the direction Paul had gone with the little girl, Caroline.

All my covering up. Gutting my friendships. Blowing my police career to smithereens. I had actually blackmailed the district attorney, hadn't I?

I covered my mouth with my hands.

I had nothing left, did I?

I made the corner. Across the busy street was some kind of park.

I looked out at a trio of street musicians and a group of old men playing chess under the trees. Other people were strolling along the path or lounging around a big white fountain. Everything was dappled with sunlight, like in that famous Renoir in all the art books.

As I came past the fountain, I spotted Paul pushing his daughter on a swing. He helped Caroline down and guided her to the sandbox as I arrived at the chain-link fence. The two of them seemed to love each other very much.

I walked around to the other end of the playground and was a few feet behind the bench Paul was sitting on when the four-year-old came running over to him.

'Daddy, Daddy!' she said.

'Yes, love?' Paul said.

'Can I have a drink?'

Paul reached into the basket of the bicycle and fished out a juice pack. I felt it in my stomach when he poked the straw through the foil. Then he knelt down and gave her another hug.

Even from behind, I could sense the joy radiating off Paul as he walked his little girl back to the swings.

'Is this seat taken?' I said as he came back to his bench.

Chapter One Hundred
and Six

At first Paul froze.

Then spasms of shock, fear, concern, and sorrow crossed his face. For a second, I thought he was going to bolt and start looking for the park exit.

Instead, he suddenly sagged down on the bench and put his head between his knees.

'Where do you want me to start?' he finally said quietly as he rubbed his temples.

'Let's see,' I said, tapping my finger against my lower lip. 'There are so many choices. How about the first time you cheated on me? Maybe the time you robbed a ticket broker at the Sheraton? Or no, no, no. The day you secretly got married. Wait, I've got it. My favorite. Tell me about the time you had a baby without me!'

Scalding tears ran down the sides of my face.

'I was barren and you needed to have a kid? Was that it? "Sorry, Lauren, you sterile waste of life. I need to be fruitful and multiply with some other woman behind your back"?'

'That wasn't it,' Paul said, looking at me, then out at his daughter. 'She was an accident.'

'You think that matters in the slightest?' I said, my face raw with anger.

Paul wiped at his eyes and looked at me.

'Just give me a second,' he said, standing. 'Then I'll tell you. I want to tell you everything.'

'How considerate,' I said.

Paul rolled the bike over to where the nannies were gathered. He spoke to one of them and then returned without the bike.

'Imelda works for the people next door. She'll take Caroline back. Why don't we walk and talk? I knew this had to happen someday.'

I shook my head. 'I didn't.'

Chapter One Hundred
and Seven

'It was almost five years ago,' Paul said as we took the strolling path at the park's perimeter.

'I picked the short straw on that bullshit analysts'-convention thing in DC, remember? I was pissed off. Things weren't going real well between me and you and ... Anyway, I was in the lounge at the Sheraton, nice room, piano bar, trying to drink away the memory of yet another ludicrous meeting, when this loud, drunken moron storms in and demands that the Patriots game be put on.'

'I want to hear about your secret family, Paul. Not some stupid hotel bar story,' I spat.

'I'm getting there,' Paul said. 'Every time there's a first down, this character has another shot of orange brandy. In the middle of the fourth quarter, he downs his eighth or ninth shot and proceeds to throw up all over the bar.

'I'm talking projectile action! As the bartender tosses him out, I look over and Veronica, who was standing on the other side of the guy, is staring at me, wide-eyed as I am. And I said, "Let's just be glad he didn't stay for the postgame celebration." That's how we met.'

'Wow, that's sweet and kind of funny,' I said with a sneer. 'You really had your groove on that night, huh?'

Paul looked at me.

'I can argue or I can explain. Not both.'

'Or get shot in the testicles,' I said. 'You left that one out.'

'Shall I continue, Lauren?' he asked.

'If you please would,' I said. 'I can't wait to hear the rest of this riveting tale.'

'So, basically, she invites me to have a drink with her. It was innocent, I swear. I wasn't trying to do anything. I don't expect you to believe that, but it's the truth. After a couple more drinks, we're just sitting there, talking, telling our life stories, and this stocky guy walks in.

'Veronica keeps staring at him, and then she says that she knows him. Turns out she used to be a Tampa Bay Buccaneers cheerleader.'

'Football?' I said, tilting my head. 'That's funny. Considering the basketballs under her shirt, I was leaning more toward the NBA.'

'She used to go out with one of the Tampa Bay assistant coaches,' Paul continued, 'and she said she remembered the guy at the bar buying Super Bowl tickets from her old boyfriend. She tells me the stocky guy is some kind of bigwig shady ticket broker. She points to the briefcase the guy is carrying and says it's probably full of hundred-dollar bills. We drink some more and talk about what we would do with that kind of money. Finally, Veronica stands up to go.'

Paul stopped walking and peered at me.

'You sure you want to hear this?'

'You want to protect my feelings now?' I said. 'Of course I want to hear the punch line.'

Paul nodded as if pained.

'"I dare you," she whispers in my ear. "I'm in two-oh-six." And off she goes.

'So, I sit and drink. Three Scotches later, I see this stocky guy get up, carrying his case. I let him leave. But then I find myself on my feet, following him. Just as a joke, I kept telling myself. No way I'm going to rob anybody. But I follow him to his room.

'Then, I don't know what got into me. I was wasted, upset, alone, and excited all at once. A couple of minutes later, I knock on the guy's door, and when he opens it, I'm punching him in the face.'

Paul and I both stepped out of the way as a bike messenger zipped between us.

'Wait a second,' I said. 'The report said you had a gun.'

Paul shook his head.

'No, we just fought. He must have made that up in order to make himself look better. He was strong. He bloodied my nose with a shot, but I was too scared to lose. I just teed off on him until he went down. Then I grabbed the briefcase, and I ran.'

'To two-oh-six?' I said.

'To two-oh-six,' Paul said with a grim nod.

Chapter One Hundred and Eight

I stumbled along the path like the sole survivor of a terrorist bombing. I remembered where we were in our marriage at the time. Not a good place. It was after we'd learned we couldn't become parents. A year of having sex like it was a science experiment. Paul having to humiliate himself with plastic cups in specialist after specialist's bathrooms. All for nothing.

We'd turned on each other then. We didn't announce it, but I could see it now, vividly. That was what had happened back then.

I decided that I couldn't care less.

I suddenly stopped short and slapped Paul. Hard! As hard as I could!

'Keep going?' he said as he rubbed his jaw.

'Good guess,' I said.

'I wake up the next morning, and at first I have no idea where I am or what's happened the night before. On the desk are two neatly divided piles of hundred-dollar bills. Veronica is sitting there in a bathrobe, pouring coffee. Fifteen minutes later, I'm walking out of her room with a gym bag full of four hundred thousand dollars.'

I shook my head. I was actually asleep, wasn't I? Dreaming this.

No, I realized. I was tripping. Somewhere along the course of this bizarre day, I'd been drugged. I rubbed my eyes. Paul goes off on a business trip and pulls off a heist?

I asked the next logical question. 'What did you do with the money?'

'Caymans,' Paul said. 'A buddy of mine on the trading desk was going down there. He set it up for me. If there's a good side to this, it's that. Four-plus years of extremely aggressive investing later, we're looking at a little over one point two million.'

I tried to let that rather large sum sink in. I was experiencing major difficulties though.

Paul continued, 'Three months after I stole the money, I get a call that puts ice in my blood. It's Veronica. She tells me she's pregnant. At first I'm insane. I tell her I want a paternity test, I want to talk to my lawyer, but she says to calm down, she's not going to boil any rabbits. She just wanted to be nice. She thought I should know that I had a child coming into the world. Whatever I wanted to do was up to me.

'So I debated, and didn't do anything for a long time, but eventually I went down to meet Caroline. One thing led to another, and well . . . One day a week, I take the shuttle down here and become Daddy.'

'For the past four years?' I said. 'Work knows about this?'

Paul shook his head.

'I just telecommute.'

'What about Veronica? You want me to believe you're not still screwing her?'

'It's true,' Paul said.

A second later, I found myself screeching with my hands around his throat. '*Bullshit!* You married her!' I screamed. 'I saw the pictures in the hall!'

Paul pulled my hands off him.

'No, no, no!' he said, holding his hands out before himself protectively as he backed away. 'That was all for Caroline's sake. We wanted her to think she has a regular daddy like everybody else. We had a photographer take some pictures. That's all. She thinks I'm a pilot.'

My eyes felt like they were filled with acid, burning deep into the sockets.

'And who does Veronica think you are?'

Paul shrugged. 'She knows who I am,' he said.

'That makes her in the minority, Paul, don't you think?' I said. 'Does she know about me?'

'From the start.'

'You fucker!' I said. I was insane with rage. I felt like biting him. 'Do *you* know who you are? Because I don't. Is your new job a bullshit story too?'

'No, that's actually real,' Paul said, suddenly sitting down on an empty bench.

'Let's face it, Lauren,' he said after a little while. 'When you and I found out we couldn't have children, our marriage started sliding badly. We both were feeling hurt, screwed up. Then you got promoted to Bronx Homicide, and that was all she wrote. Turnaround after turnaround. Double, triple shifts. Don't get me wrong, I didn't blame you. I just never saw much of you. I really didn't think there was a chance in hell of us getting back together.

'But things are so different now, Lauren. You're pregnant. It was like somebody hit a "pause" button, then remembered the two of us after four years and just hit "play" again. Caroline is in my heart, but I'd be willing to give up even her for you. There's an actual "us" again, a future. I'm ready to do anything for that.'

Paul gripped my hand.

'I've always just wanted us. You know that. From the first time I set eyes on you. We can work it out, Lauren. This . . . shit –

it's just a stupid, horrible detour. All the lies are over now.'

'That sounds really sweet, Paul,' I said, pulling my hand away. 'Really wonderful and nice, except for one thing. One small detail.'

He looked at me quizzically. Now it was my turn to hurt him. Let's see how he liked getting his heart napalmed.

'You left something out. Something really important. The cop I watched you kill. I was there when you killed Scott, dumbass.'

Chapter One Hundred and Nine

Paul's face seemed to crumple in front of me. 'You were *where*?' he asked.

'At Scott's place in Riverdale,' I told him. 'You must have read our e-mails, but guess what? You were too late. He'd just been with me, Paul. Right before you cracked his skull open, we'd been in bed together. Turnabout is fair play, no? So how does it feel?'

Apparently not too good. Paul's mouth was gaping wider than *The Scream*'s. 'So you were . . . How did . . .' he stammered.

'That's right, Paul,' I said. 'Surprise, surprise.'

I grabbed his wrist, squeezed with all my might.

'Who the hell do you think has been keeping you out of jail all this time? Your fairy godmother? I covered things up for you, destroyed my career – everything I was – in order to keep you out of prison. I actually felt sorry for you. Can you imagine that?'

Paul put his hand out toward my face. I slapped it down.

Other strollers started making a wide berth around us.

'And come to think of it,' I snarled, 'how dare you kill Scott when you knew you were being unfaithful to me? Who the hell are you? Thief. Murderer. Bigamist. What am I missing?'

I slapped him again, and it felt so good.

'Scott had a wife and three kids!'

Paul broke my grip, then walked away. He stood on the other side of the path so that I wouldn't hit him again, I assumed. After a while, he did something astounding. *He started laughing.*

'You want to let me in on the joke?' I said, red-faced, walking toward him. 'I could use a real rib-tickler right around now.'

Paul turned to me.

'Sure,' he said. 'Here's the punch line: I didn't kill Scott because he was sleeping with you. I had no idea about that, Lauren.'

He folded his arms across his chest and gave me another smile. I didn't get it, not a word he was saying.

'I killed him because he was blackmailing me,' said Paul.

Chapter One Hundred and Ten

N ow it was my turn to put my head down between my knees. 'Blackmailing you?' I asked.

Paul nodded.

'A year ago, Veronica came up to New York. She has a friend who's a model or something who gets her work. Eleven o'clock in the morning, she finds herself in the middle of a drug raid, and I get this frantic call at work to go and try to help her out.

'I walk into this apartment down in SoHo, expecting a million cops, but there's only one. *Scott Thayer.* I'd gotten there too late, though, because Veronica got scared and told him we had money. He takes me into the kitchen and tells me he's a reasonable guy. He'll let everybody go free for ten grand cash.'

I felt a sharp pain in my neck. My skin felt clammy.

'So I gave it to him,' Paul said. 'A month goes by. One day I'm coming back to my desk after lunch, and Thayer's sitting at it, holding a picture of you. He tells me that you two work out of the same precinct house, and for *another* twenty grand, not only will he not turn me in – nice guy that he is – he won't tell you about Veronica.'

Paul looked at me. I stared back at him, my mouth gaping.

'So I give him that. It was when he came back the third time that I realized it would never end. He wanted fifty thousand. Instead of giving it to him, I decided I'd rather take a shot at wrapping things up my own way.'

I listened to flute music from somewhere in the park. It sounded like a dirge at my own funeral.

I'd thought Paul had fought for me. That his killing Scott had been about me. But it was over money, blackmail.

'You understand that Thayer wasn't content to keep on black-mailing me,' Paul continued. 'He wanted all of it. He came after you to get another hook into me. That's all he wanted with you, Lauren.'

'So you killed him?' I said bitterly. 'You're a gangster now? Robbing people and shooting cops. Maybe you should cut a rap album.'

Paul squinted down at the ground, then shrugged. 'Things just kind of kept on happening. One thing led to another.'

A scintilla of compassion rose inside me. The same thing had happened to me, hadn't it? I pushed the sympathy away as quickly as I could. The last thing I would do was feel sorry for Paul.

'Listen, Lauren,' Paul said. 'Why don't we call it the mother of all midlife crises? I'll do whatever you want now. Give the money back. Or we can just go. We'll drive to Reagan International straight from here. A million point two dollars tax free is a lot of money. Why don't we just go and spend it? Raise our kid on a sailboat. You're mad now, but you betrayed me too, remember? Let's just . . . go. C'mon, Lauren. We can do this together.'

Chapter One Hundred and Eleven

I sat there, staring at my incredible conman of a husband. What an amazing liar he was. Then I dropped my eyes to the pavement, my shoulders slumping. The world seemed to slow suddenly, the music in the air, the sound of traffic.

It was official. I had given Paul everything that I possibly could. My love, my work, my reputation. And now I had absolutely zero left.

I was still sitting there, agonizing, when Paul's daughter appeared again. The nanny Paul had spoken to stood waiting a few feet away with another toddler and Caroline's bike.

'Daddy!' she said. 'Pictures! I want to show Imelda the pictures.'

'Not now, love,' Paul called to the girl. 'Later, sweetheart.'

'But they're my brothers,' the girl said, pulling a black-and-white photograph out of Paul's jacket before he could stop her. It fell to the ground as he tried to snatch it back.

'You're mean, Daddy,' the four-year-old said with a pout. 'I want Imelda to see the picture of my new twin brothers.'

My eyes strained in their sockets. *What!*

Paul stared down at the small square photograph, his Adam's apple bobbing.

'Show her later, Caroline,' he snapped. Imelda took one look at him before quickly grabbing Caroline's hand and pulling her away.

I bent and lifted the precious picture off the pavement. I nodded once, twice.

It showed a sonogram. Two fetuses. Twins. I pictured Veronica again. Of course she looked like she'd recently put on weight. She was pregnant!

I looked at Paul's face, almost with fascination. He'd lied so effortlessly to me. Again and again.

He would never stop, I realized. There was something deeply, incredibly wrong with Paul. He would say anything, do anything. How could anyone tell lies like this? How could anyone do the awful things he'd done? Even the way he'd just snarled at his little girl. I'd protected a monster.

'I know exactly what we're going to do now,' I said, letting the black-and-white picture fall to the cobblestones. 'What I should have done when this whole thing started.'

I whisked out my cuffs and snapped them on to his wrists. 'Paul, you're under arrest.'

Chapter One Hundred
and Twelve

Nannies, chess players, and joggers were outright gaping as I dragged a handcuffed Paul out of the park. Of course they looked at us. Good God, he was twice my size.

'You sure this is the right thing to do, Lauren?' he whined as I perp-walked him two long blocks back toward my Taurus. 'A million dollars? You still love me or you wouldn't have covered for me. Which isn't going to go well for you, either. You'll get charged as an accessory to murder. The baby will be born behind bars. You're not really thinking this through.'

'Unfortunately for you, Paul, I'm tired of thinking,' I said. 'Thinking is what got me into this mess. I'm just doing what's right. Trying to, anyway.'

I stopped suddenly as we passed Paul's parallel-parked Jaguar. 'Where are the keys, Paul? Let's end it in style. Give me a taste of that million dollars. Maybe I'll change my mind and drive to the airport.'

I jabbed him in the small of his back. 'But don't bet on it.'

I took the keys from his jacket pocket and then pushed him into the passenger seat. I went around to the other side. I was sliding the key into the ignition when Paul popped open the glove compartment.

A second later, I felt something hard sticking under my right armpit.

'Time to cut all the bullshit, Lauren,' Paul said, digging a small revolver into my ribs.

Idiot! I thought. Of course he had a gun. The ticket broker hadn't lied about that. Paul had.

'Hey, I thought you said you didn't have a gun,' I said.

'You still haven't picked up on the theme here, Lauren,' Paul said. 'I tell you only what you need to hear. Now get the cuffs off me. *Right now!*'

'Then what? You're going to shoot me?' I said as I did what he asked. I didn't have a choice. 'Might as well, Paul. You've done everything else to me.'

'Hey, you're the one who started this game. Slapping cuffs on me,' Paul said.

'That's what you think this is, don't you?' I said. 'Some kind of game? News flash, Paul. You killed a man. You're a mur-der-er.'

Paul's face scrunched in rage. He turned bright red, his eyes glittering with fury.

'News flash? Let me tell you something. You know what it's like to have a wife with bigger balls than you? While you were out kicking ass, I was busy downtown *kissing* asses, so you could have nice things. But that's JUST NOT GOOD ENOUGH FOR YOU!!!'

Paul pistol-whipped the dashboard savagely, then pressed the gun barrel to my temple.

'You want to know how I felt when Veronica made me that offer at the Sheraton? For the first time, I felt like a man! I got a chance to step away from this namby-pamby investment firm, law degree, 401K bullshit I've been wasting my whole life on.'

Paul took a deep breath, then released it. The gun stayed at my temple.

'I did it, Lauren,' he whispered fiercely. 'I took what I wanted, and then I went and got my prize. Let me tell you something. I remember every second of it. And Lauren, it was good. Veronica licked the blood off my knuckles. I knocked her up like a stud bull.'

'Anything you say, psychopath,' I said.

'And you're right. I killed that prick Scott. He thought he could just keep messing with me. You should have seen the look on his face when he turned around. He was outmanned, and he knew it. I gave your boyfriend exactly what was coming to him. I could give two shits about his wife and kids.'

In the distance, sirens sounded. Somebody must have called the police about the scene Paul and I were making. Thank God for cell phones!

'You hear that?' I said. 'Sirens? That's the sound of truth and consequences catching up with you, Paul.'

'Nothing is catching up with me, cupcake,' Paul said, opening the door and shoving me out. 'Time for a trial separation.'

The Jag's tires smoked as he peeled out on to Riggs.

I stood between the skid marks, disoriented. Could somebody please tell me what the hell had just happened? The past few hours seemed impossible, surreal. What was I thinking, hours. Try the last few minutes.

My hair flew back in the wake of two siren-wailing DC police cars that appeared in full-speed pursuit of Paul.

This was it? I thought. *This was how it would end?*

Half a block north across the street, I spotted my rental car.

Not if I could help it, I thought, taking out the keys as I ran.

Chapter One Hundred and Thirteen

Minutes later, I was pinning the gas, tailgating the rear DC cop car that was chasing Paul. I felt like giving him my brights. Gangway! NYPD coming through! Paul is mine. Get in line! That's my cheating, lying, murdering husband trying to get away.

We careened through another ritzy neighborhood. Were we in Georgetown? Ivy-covered brick and Greek revivals blurred past my windshield. Where did Paul think he was going? Did he still believe he could get away with this?

I figured it all out when I spotted the tower of the bridge back to the airport. It loomed a half-mile away, above some slate roofs on my left.

I whipped a left at the next corner, ran a red light, and screeched a right on to M Street, speeding toward the bridge to cut him off if I could.

I honked as I skidded to a stop – dead center at the entrance to the Francis Scott Key Bridge.

Then I jumped out of the car and stood in the open doorway.

'Get your crazy ass out of the street!' an angry bus driver screamed at me as he leaned on his horn. 'What in the green world of God do you think you're doing?'

You think I know? I felt like telling him. But I didn't have the energy or the time.

A block to the north, Paul was approaching with the DC cops close behind. When he reached the traffic I'd just backed up, he put the Jaguar up on the sidewalk. No hesitation. A hot dog cart and newspaper box sailed off the Jaguar's grill before Paul bulleted into the intersection.

I jumped to the left of my Taurus, filling the only space that might fit Paul's car. The bus driver screamed as the Jag sped toward me. I was the only thing standing between Paul and the bridge.

I stood there transfixed.

Paul would stop.

He wouldn't run me down.

He couldn't kill me.

The car kept coming, though. Really fast.

At the last second, I dove to the right.

The Jag blew past me like a hunter-green guided missile. Twisting around on my back, I watched Paul slalom around my car and back on to the bridge road. Son of a bitch was going to make it. He would have run me down – no problem at all.

But then his right back wheel caught the curb with a savage pop, and the car went airborne.

An amazing sight.

There was a deafening crunch, a sound like a giant plastic bottle being fed into a recycling machine, as the Jaguar collided with a concrete bridge abutment.

Glass hung in the air like dust motes as the Jag accordioned. Then the ruined car flipped end over end, snapping through riverside trees before exploding into the muddy green water of the Potomac.

Chapter One Hundred
and Fourteen

The Jaguar had disappeared – and Paul with it.

I tripped on a partially buried shopping cart as I half ran, half fell down the embankment. Now what? Well, I did an awkward triple lutz before I belly flopped painfully into the river. Then I kicked my way straight down, scanning the murky water for the Jag and Paul.

I don't know why I was being so brave, foolish – whatever this ought to be called. Maybe because it was the right thing to do.

I was about to go back up for more air when I spotted a shard of twisted metal. I swam toward it.

No!

It was the Jag. Paul was still belted into his seat behind the deployed air bag.

His eyes were closed, his face stitched with bleeding cuts. How long had he been in the water? When did brain damage start? I thought, yanking open the car door.

I leaned across Paul, struggling desperately against the air bag to undo his shoulder belt. The damn thing wouldn't open.

Then I felt his hands bite into my neck.

What was he doing?

My throat was already burning. I couldn't believe this. I guess I was the one with the brain damage! Here I was, trying to save him – and he wanted to kill me at the bottom of the Potomac. Paul really was crazy.

River water burned my nasal cavity as I struggled. Very soon I would be out of strength and oxygen. Then what? That was simple – *I would drown.*

I kept fighting against him, but that wasn't working. Paul was too big, too strong. I had to go another way. And fast!

I pushed hard against the windshield. Then I shot my elbow back, catching Paul in the throat. Then I did it again!

The pressure on my neck let up as an air bubble the size of Rhode Island blobbed out of Paul's mouth. I ducked from beneath his arms. I felt myself starting to pass out, though.

Paul grabbed my foot as I struggled to turn away from him. He was still stuck in the car, his open eyes bulging. He was going to take me with him, if it was the last thing he did, which it would be.

I kicked forward against the water, then straight back into his nose. *I broke it for sure.* Blood blossomed around his face. Then his grip let free, and I kicked myself away from the car, up toward the light.

I looked back and could see Paul's face below. He was bleeding, and he seemed to be screaming. Then he was gone.

I broke the surface and gorged myself on blessed air as the strong river current pulled me along. Up on a bridge I floated under, there were spinning police lights and dozens of staring faces. The riverside trees swayed in a police helicopter's rotor wash.

A fireman shouted and tossed me a life preserver. I grabbed it and held on for dear life.

Chapter One Hundred and Fifteen

The DC cops took real good care of me after that. They had checked our flight list, assumed Paul and I were on vacation and that he had simply snapped.

I didn't say anything to change their mind. In fact, after I ID'd the body, I didn't say anything at all.

An hour later, my buddy Detective Zampella himself arrived at the scene and managed to squash the story with the local media. Then Zampella got me the hell out of there.

I needed to crash somewhere. But not in DC.

I didn't want to fly, so I got in my rental and drove all the way to Baltimore before the urge to rest came over me again.

I remembered staying at a nice Sheraton near the inner harbor one time, and I found the hotel on Charles Street.

The Sheraton Inner Harbor Hotel. Never has any hotel looked better to me.

I got a room with a water view, instead of one overlooking Oriole Park at Camden Yards. Not that I really cared right now.

The room was all blues and creams and it was definitely what I needed, because I was the ultimate frazzled traveler.

The bed was sweet, just terrific, and I spent the rest of the evening motionless, almost comatose, staring up at the ceiling. As the numbness started to wear off, I felt sad, angry, anxious, ashamed, and helpless all at once. Finally, I slept.

The next time I looked up, it was still dark. I stared at the walls of the strange room, not remembering where I was at first. It all came back to me as I glanced out the window and saw the lit-up harbor. A big boat called *The Chesapeake*. Baltimore – *the Sheraton Inner Harbor*.

Then other images came.

Paul. Veronica. Little blonde Caroline.

The Jaguar in the Potomac.

I lay in the dark and thought it all through from the beginning. What I had done. How I felt about it now. How I felt about myself. I pinched my eyes shut. Vivid sensations and memories flashed through me periodically. The smell of Scott's cologne. The taste of rain in his kiss. The feel of the rain on my shins as I stared at his battered body. Paul in the Jaguar at the end.

My breath caught at what I remembered next.

I saw silver-white light streaming through the windows of the church where Paul and I were married. My left hand twitched as I felt the slide of a gold ring.

The despair that overtook me then was like a seizure. I felt like it was something that had always been in me. Some dark blossom that had been waiting to bloom since the day I was married.

For the next two hours I did nothing but cry.

Eventually I found a phone and ordered a sandwich and beer from the Orioles Grill in the hotel. I turned on the TV. On the eleven o'clock news there was a lurid shot of the bridge in DC where the accident occurred, and of Paul's car being lifted from the river.

I was about to cry again, but I stopped myself with deep, hard breaths. Enough of that for now. I shook my head at the screen as the news anchor called it a tragic accident.

'You don't know the half of it,' I said. 'You have no idea what you're talking about, mister. No idea.'

EPILOGUE

Chapter One Hundred
and Sixteen

The last few minutes of my hour-long run were always the bear. I kept my eyes focused on the silver lap of water on sand, the slight give of the wet dirt under the balls of my feet.

As I finished my kick, I dropped to the beach, lungs burning, amazed at what I'd just accomplished. *Five miles – on sand.*

For the umpteenth morning in a row, the sun broke above the horizon, and I witnessed the miracle moment when the water and the seashore became gold.

I stared along the curving rim of beach I'd just run. It was like a gilded crescent moon laid on its side. Darn pretty.

I checked my watch. *You're gonna be late, Lauren.*

I found my moped in the near-empty parking lot. I put on my flip-flops, then helmet. Safety first. I nodded at a couple of fishermen who looked familiar, swerved around wolf-whistling, sun-browned surfers in a canary-yellow convertible, and hit the winding beach road toward town.

Funny how things work out, I thought as I buzzed along the narrow ribbon of asphalt.

The FedEx package had arrived three months to the day after Paul's death. Inside was a letter. It was typed on expensive stationery, the letterhead from an attorney of the Cayman Islands Trust Bank.

Paul had left the stolen money plus interest, $1,257,000.22 – in my name.

Didn't matter, I still wasn't ready to forgive him.

I was tempted to turn it in, maybe give it to some charity. But by then I was coming along, and there's nothing like a baby's kick to make you realize it isn't about you anymore. I did send $250,000 of the money to the Thayer family, but that was just me doing the right thing. Doing the best I could, anyway.

I pulled into the short drive of a glass house perched on a cliff above the beach. With its leaking roof and rusty sliders, it was more glass trailer than house, but you couldn't beat the view, or the privacy.

I left my bike helmet on as I ran inside. I needed to check in on the man in my life.

My baby boy exploded into giggles as I knelt in front of his snuggly bouncer. How do you like that? I was still a sucker for younger men.

His name was Thomas. After my dad, who else?

A Spanish woman clucked at me from the kitchen doorway.

'What are you doing here, Miss Lauren?' she said. 'You can't miss your first day of work.'

'I just thought I'd give Tommy one more kiss and a hug,' I said.

She pointed at the front door.

'*Basta*,' she said. 'You may come back for lunch. And to see Thomas. Now, *vamanos*.'

Chapter One Hundred and Seventeen

My office space was only ten minutes away, just above a popular bar on a busy tourist street.

I climbed the stairs and undid my chin strap as I gaped at the new 'Paradise Investigations' sign above the weathered door. *This is good. Looks right, feels right.*

I went back down the stairs and into the bar – wading my way through the jungle path of tikis and palms.

The bartender turned the page of last Sunday's *New York Daily News* and looked up at me.

My old partner, Mike Ortiz, rolled his eyes before he smiled broadly – the only way Mike can smile.

'Hey, gumshoe,' he said. 'Aren't you supposed to be shadowing some nasty hombre, or something like that? And what did I tell you about my aunt Rosa? If you keep going back home, she'll think you don't trust her with little Thomas.'

We could have been sitting next to each other in our old squad car, except Mike was wearing a Hawaiian shirt that looked like it might require batteries. He seemed to have adjusted pretty well to life after The Job, anyway.

He'd told me to look him up, and that's what I did. It wasn't like I had anywhere else to go. Besides, Mike was just about the only honest man I knew. And actually kind of cute, I was starting to notice.

'I saw your new shingle upstairs,' Mike said. 'Real nice. Except you do know this is a Spanish-speaking country, don't you? How much business do you think you're going to get with a sign in English?'

'As little as possible, dummy,' I said, stealing the Style section. 'What does a girl have to do to get a cup of joe around here?'

'Let me think about it,' Mike said, 'while I get you that coffee.'

Then he added, apropos of nothing really, 'You're doing real good, Lauren. You and Thomas.'

I blushed down to my toes. I guess I'm just not used to compliments yet.